Amelia Ann Blanford Edwards

Half a million of money

In three Volumes. Vol. I

Amelia Ann Blanford Edwards

Half a million of money
In three Volumes. Vol. I

ISBN/EAN: 9783744741132

Printed in Europe, USA, Canada, Australia, Japan

Cover: Foto ©Andreas Hilbeck / pixelio.de

More available books at **www.hansebooks.com**

HALF A MILLION OF MONEY.

A Novel.

BY

AMELIA B. EDWARDS,

AUTHOR OF "BARBARA'S HISTORY," ETC., ETC.

"O Bella età dell' oro!"—GUARINI.

IN THREE VOLUMES.
VOL. I.

LONDON :

TINSLEY BROTHERS, 18, CATHERINE ST., STRAND.
1866.

[*The Right of Translation is reserved.*]

BRADBURY, EVANS, AND CO., PRINTERS, WHITEFRIARS.

CONTENTS.

HALF A MILLION OF MONEY.

PROLOGUE. A.D. 1760.

JACOB TREFALDEN, merchant and alderman of London, lay dying in an upper chamber of his house in Basinghall-street, towards evening on the twenty-second day of March, Anno Domini seventeen hundred and sixty.

It was growing rapidly dusk. The great house was full of gloom, and silence, and the shadow of death. Two physicians occupied two easy-chairs before the fire in the sick man's chamber. They were both notabilities in their day. The one was Sir John Pringle, Physician Extraordinary to the King—a brave and skilful man who had smelt powder at Dettingen, and won the soldiers' hearts by his indomitable coolness under fire. The

other was Doctor Joshua Ward, commonly called
" Spot Ward " from his rubicund face, and im-
mortalised by Hogarth in that bitter caricature
called "The Company of Undertakers."

These gentlemen did little in the way of
conversation. When they spoke at all, it was
in a whisper. Now and then, they compared
their watches with the time-piece on the mantelshelf. Now and then, they glanced towards the
bed, where, propped almost upright with pillows,
an old man was sinking gradually out of life.
There was something very ghastly in that old
man's face, purple-hued, unconscious, and swathed
in wet bandages. His eyes were closed. His
lips were swollen. His breathing was slow and
stertorous. He had been smitten down that day
at noon by a stroke of apoplexy; was carried
home from 'Change in a dying state; and had
not spoken since. His housekeeper crouched by
his bed-side, silent and awestruck. His three
sons and his lawyer waited in the drawing-room
below. They all knew that he had not two more
hours to live.

In the meantime the dusk thickened, and the

evening stillness grew more and more oppressive.
A chariot rumbled past from time to time, or a
newsvender trudged by, hawking the London
Gazette, and proclaiming the progress of Lord
George Sackville's trial.   Sometimes a neighbour's footboy came to the door with a civil
inquiry; or a little knot of passengers loitered
on the opposite pavement, and glanced up,
whisperingly, at the curtained windows.   By-
and-by, even these ceased to come and go.   A
few oil-lamps were lighted at intervals along the
dingy thoroughfare, and the stars and the watch-
men came out together.

"In the name of Heaven," said Captain
Trefalden, "let us have lights!"—and rang the
drawing-room bell.

Candles were brought, and the heavy damask
curtains were drawn.   Captain Trefalden took
up the Gazette   Frederick Trefalden looked at
himself in the glass, arranged the folds of his
cravat, yawned, took snuff, and contemplated the
symmetry of his legs; William Trefalden drew
his chair to the table, and began abstractedly
turning over the leaves of the last "Idler."   There

were other papers and books on the table as well
—among them a little volume called "Rasselas,"
from the learned pen of Mr. Samuel Johnson (he
was not yet LL.D.), and the two first volumes
of "Tristram Shandy," written by that ingenious
gentleman, the Reverend Laurence Sterne. Both
works were already popular, though published
only a few months before.

These three brothers were curiously alike, and
curiously unlike. They all resembled their father;
they were all fine men; and they were all good-
looking. Old Jacob was a Cornish man, had
been fair and stalwart in his youth, and stood five
feet eleven without his shoes. Captain Trefalden
was not so fair; Frederick Trefalden was not so
tall; William Trefalden was neither so fair, nor
so tall, nor so handsome; and yet they were all
like him, and like each other.

Captain Jacob was the eldest. His father had
intended him for his own business; but, somehow or another, the lad never took kindly to
indigo. He preferred scarlet—especially scarlet
turned up with buff—and he went into the army.
Having led a roving, irregular youth; sown his

wild oats in various congenial European soils; and fought gallantly at Dettingen, Fontenoy, Laffeldt, and Minden, he had now, at forty years of age, committed the unspeakable folly of marrying for neither rank nor money, but only for love. His father had threatened to disinherit Captain Trefalden for this misdeed, and for five months past had forbidden him the house. His brothers were even more indignant than their father—or had seemed to be so. In short, this was the first occasion on which the worthy officer had set foot in Basinghall-street for many a long day; and all three gentlemen were naturally somewhat constrained and silent.

Frederick, the second son, was thirty-six; William, thirty. Frederick hated indigo almost as cordially as his brother Jacob; William had scarcely a thought that was not dyed in it. Frederick was an airy, idle, chocolate-drinking, snuff-taking, card-playing, ridotto-haunting man of pleasure. William was a cool, methodical, ambitious man of business. Neither of the three had ever cared much for the other two. It was not in the nature of things that much affection should exist between them. Their temperaments and pursuits were radically unlike. They had lost their mother while they were yet boys. They had never had a sister. The sweet womanly home-links had all been wanting to bind their hearts together.

And now the brothers were met under their father's roof, this memorable twenty-second evening in March; and in the dark chamber overhead, already beyond all help from human skill, that father lay dying. They were all thinking the same thoughts in the silence of their hearts, and in those thoughts there was neither prayer nor sadness. Poor old man! He was immensely rich—he was pitiably destitute. No one loved him; and he was worth Half a Million of Money.

Mr. Frederick Trefalden took out his watch, swore a fashionable oath, and declared that he was famishing.

"Have somewhat to eat, brother Fred," suggested the captain; and so rang the bell again, and ordered refreshments to be taken into the dining-room.

The two younger Trefaldens exchanged glances

and a covert smile. Their elder brother was already assuming the master, it should seem! Well, well, Lawyer Beavington is there, and the will has yet to be read.

In the meantime Mr. Fred and the captain go down together; for the latter has ridden up from Hounslow, and will not object to join his brother in "a snack of cold meat and a bumper of claret." Mr. Will, like a sober citizen, has dined at two o'clock, and only desires that a dish of tea may be sent to him in the drawing-room.

If anything could be more dismal than that gloomy drawing-room it was the still gloomier dining-room below. The walls were panelled with dark oak, richly carved. The chimney-piece was a ponderous cenotaph in black and yellow marble. The hangings were of mulberry-coloured damask. A portrait of the master of the house, painted forty years before by Sir James Thornhill, hung over the fireplace. Seen by the feeble glimmer of a couple of wax lights, there was an air of sepulchral magnificence about the place which was infinitely depressing. The very viands might have reminded these gentlemen of

funeral-baked meats—above all, the great veal
pasty, which lay in state in the middle of the
board.   They were both hungry, however, and it
did nothing of the kind.

The captain took his place at the head of the
table, and plunged his knife gallantly into the
heart of the pasty.

"If thou hast as good a stomach, Fred, as
myself," said he, growing cordial under the influence of the good things before him, "I'll warrant thee we'll sack this fortress handsomely!"

The fine gentleman shrugged his shoulders
somewhat contemptuously.

"I detest such coarse dishes," said he.   "I
dined with Sir Harry Fanshawe yesterday at the
Hummums.   We had a ragout of young chicks
not a week out of the shell, and some à-la-mode
beef that would have taken thy breath away,
brother Jacob."

"I'd as lieve eat of this pasty as of any ragout
in Christendom," said the captain.

"Mr. Horace Walpole and Mrs. Clive were at
dinner all the time in the next room," continued
the beau; "and the drollest part of the story is

that Sir Harry and I adjourned in the evening to
Vauxhall, and there, by Jove! found ourselves
supping in the very next box to Mr. Horace and
Mrs. Kitty again!"

"Help yourself to claret, Fred—and pass the
bottle," said the captain, who, strange to say, saw
no point in the story at all.

"Not bad wine," observed Mr. Fred, tasting
his claret with the air of a connoisseur. "The
old gentleman hath an excellent cellar."

"Ay, indeed," replied the captain, thoughtfully.

"But he never knew how to enjoy his money."

"Never."

"To live in a place like this, for instance," said
the beau, looking round the room. "Basinghall-
street—faugh! And to keep such a cook; and
never to have set up his chariot! 'Sdeath, sir,
you and I will know better what to do with the
guineas!"

"I should think so, brother Fred, I should
think so," replied the captain, with a touch of
sadness in his voice, "'Twas a dull life—poor
old gentleman! Methinks you and I might have
helped to make it gayer."

"Curse me, if I know how!" ejaculated Mr. Fred.

"By sticking to the business—by living at home—by doing like young Will, yonder," replied the elder brother. "That boy hath been a better son than you or I, brother Fred."

Mr. Fred looked very grave indeed. "Will hath an old head on young shoulders," said he. "Harkee, Jacob, hast any notion how the old man hath bestowed his money?"

"No more than this glass of claret," replied the captain.

They were both silent. A footstep went by in the hall. They listened; they looked at each other; they filled their glasses again. The same thought was uppermost in the mind of each.

"The fairest thing, Fred," said the honest captain; "would be, if 'twere left to us, share and share alike."

"Share and share alike!" echoed Mr. Fred, with a sounding oath. "Nay; the old man was too proud of his fortune to do that, brother Jacob. My own notion of this matter is—— hush! Any one listening?"

Captain Trefalden rose, glanced into the hall, closed the door, and resumed his seat.

"Not a soul. Well?"

"Well, my own notion is, that we younger sons shall have a matter of sixty or eighty thousand apiece; while you, as the head of the family, will take the bulk."

"It may be, Fred," mused the captain, complacently.

"And that bulk," continued Mr. Fred, "will be some three hundred and forty thousand pounds."

"I shall have to ask thee, Fred, how to spend it," said the captain, smiling.

"Then thou shalt spend it like a prince. Thou shalt buy an estate in Kent, and a town-house in Soho; thou shalt have horses, chariots, lacqueys, liveries, wines, a pack of hounds, a box at the Italian Opera ..."

"Of which I don't understand a word," interrupted the captain.

"A French cook, a private chaplain, a black footboy, a suite of diamonds for thy wife, and for thyself the prettiest mistress ..."

"Hold, Fred," interposed the captain again.
"None of the last, I beseech thee. My days of
gallantry are over."

"But, my dear brother, no man of quality . . ."

"I'm not a man of quality," said the other.
"I'm a simple soldier, and the son of a plain
City merchant."

"Well, then, no man of parts and fortune . . ."

"The fortune's not mine yet, Fred," said the
captain, dryly. "And as for my parts, why, I
think the less said of them the better. I'm no
scholar, and that thou knowest as well as myself.
Hark! some one taps. Come in."

The door opened, and a bronzed upright man,
with something of a military bearing, came in.
He held his hat and cane in his hand, and saluted
the brothers courteously. It was Sir John
Pringle.

"Gentlemen," he said, gravely, "I grieve to be
the bearer of sad tidings."

The brothers rose in silence. Captain Trefalden
changed colour.

"Is he—is my father dead?" he faltered.

The physician bent his head.

Captain Trefalden turned his face away, Frederick Trefalden took out his handkerchief, and ostentatiously wiped away a tear—which was not there.

"Dr. Ward is gone," said Sir John, after a brief pause. "He desired his respects and condolences. Gentlemen, I wish you a good evening."

"You will take a glass of claret, Sir John?" said Mr. Fred, pressing forward to the table. But almost before he could say the words, the physician had waved a civil negative, and was gone. Mr. Fred shrugged his shoulders, filled the glass all the same, and emptied it.

"Zounds, brother," said he, "'tis of no use to be melancholy. Remember thou'rt now the head of the family. Let us go up-stairs and read the will."

In the meantime, William Trefalden, like a methodical young man of business, had been up to his father's room to find his father's keys, and down to the counting-house to fetch his father's deed-box out from the iron-safe. When Mr. Fred and the captain came into the room, they found Lawyer Beavington with his spectacles on, and the box before him.

"Gentlemen," he said, with calm importance, "be pleased to sit."

So the brothers drew their chairs to the table, and sat down ; all silent ; all somewhat agitated.

The man of law unlocked the box.

It was full of papers, leases, transfers, debentures, agreements, bills of exchange, and so forth. These had all to be taken out, opened, and laid aside before the will turned up. That important document lay at the very bottom, like hope at the bottom of Pandora's casket.

"'Tis not a long will," observed Mr. Beavington, with a preparatory cough.

As he unfolded it, a slip of paper fell out.

"A memorandum, apparently, in your excellent father's own hand," said he, glancing through it. "Hm—ha—refers to the amount of his fortune. Have you, gentlemen, framed any ideas of the extent of the property ? "

"'Twas thought my father owned half a million of money," replied Mr. Fred, eagerly.

"More than that," said the youngest son, with a shake of the head.

"You are right, sir. The memorandum runs thus: *'Upon a rough calculation, I believe I may estimate my present estate at about five hundred and twenty-five thousand pounds. (Dated) January the first, Anno Domini seventeen hundred and sixty. Jacob Trefalden.'* A goodly fortune, gentlemen —a goodly fortune! "

The three brothers drew a deep breath of satisfaction.

"Five hundred and twenty-five thousand pounds!" repeated the captain. "Prythee, Mr. Beavington, proceed to the will."

The lawyer folded up the memorandum very slowly, drew the candles nearer, wiped his spectacles, and began.

"'In the name of GOD, AMEN. I JACOB TREFALDEN born in the town of Redruth in the County of Cornwall and now a citizen of London, Merchant (a Widower) being at present in good health of Body, and of sound and disposing Mind and Memory, for which I bless GOD, Do this eleventh day of January one thousand seven hundred and sixty make and ordain this my last Will and Testament in manner and form following (that it is to say) IMPRIMIS I DESIRE to be interred in my Family Vault by the side of my lately deceased wife and with as little Pomp and ceremony as may be. ITEM I give to such of my Executors hereinafter named as shall act under this my Will Five Hundred pounds Sterling each to be paid to or retained by them within six Calendar Months after my decease. I GIVE to my three sons Jacob, Frederick and William Five Thousand pounds Sterling each. I GIVE . . . '"

"Stay! five thou—— please to read that again, Mr. Beavington," interrupted Captain Trefalden.

"Five Thousand pounds Sterling each," repeated the lawyer. "The amount is quite plain. But have patience, gentlemen. We are but at the preliminaries. This five thousand each hath, doubtless, some special purpose. The main business is to come."

"Very possibly—very possibly, Mr. Beavington," replied the captain. "I am all attention."

"'ITEM I GIVE to my Cashier Edward Prescott Five Hundred pounds Sterling. I GIVE to my other clerks One Hundred pounds Sterling each. AND I GIVE to my Household Servants Two Hundred pounds Sterling, to be divided among them in equal shares. All which last mentioned legacies I direct shall be paid within three Calendar Months next after my decease. I GIVE to the Minister for the time being of Redruth aforesaid and to the Minister for the time being of the Parish in which I shall happen to reside immediately previous to my decease One Hundred pounds Sterling each to be paid to them within One Calendar Month after that event shall happen and be by them forthwith distributed in such manner and proportion as they shall think proper among the poor Widows belonging to their Parishes respectively. ITEM, I do hereby direct and appoint that my Executors shall as soon as possible after my decease set apart out of my Property which consists entirely of Personal Estate, and is chiefly invested in the Government Stocks and Funds of this Kingdom, so much of my Funded property as shall be equal in value to

the sum of Five Hundred Thousand pounds
Sterling . . .'"

"Ha! now for it!" exclaimed Mr. Fred,
breathlessly.

"'——the sum of Five Hundred Thousand
pounds Sterling,'" continued the lawyer, "'which
I give to the Lord Mayor and Aldermen of the
City of London for the time being and their
successors for ever IN TRUST for the purposes
hereinafter expressed, and I desire that as to
this Gift they shall be called "TREFALDEN'S
TRUSTEES," and that the amount of my Funded
Property so to be set apart shall immediately
afterwards be transferred to them accordingly.'"

The lawyer paused to clear his glasses. The
brothers looked blankly in each other's faces.

"Good God! Mr. Beavington," gasped Captain
Trefalden, "what does this mean?"

"On my word, sir, I have no more notion than
yourself," replied the lawyer. "The will is none
of my making."

"Who drew it up?" asked Mr. Will, per-
emptorily.

"Not I, sir. Your father hath gone to some

stranger for this business.   But perchance when
we know more——"

"Enough, sir, go on," said Mr. Fred and Mr.
Will together.

The lawyer continued :

"'AND I hereby declare my Will to be that
my said Trustees shall receive the annual Income
of the said Trust Fund, and lay out and invest
such Income in their names in the Purchase of
Government Securities, and repeat such receipts
and Investments from time to time in the nature
of Compound Interest during the space of One
Hundred years from the date of my decease, and
that such accumulations shall continue and be
increased until the same, with the original Trust
Fund, shall amount to, and become in the aggre-
gate, one entire clear principal sum of NINE
MILLION POUNDS Sterling and upwards,
AND I DESIRE that the same entire clear
Principal Sum shall thenceforth be, or be con-
sidered as, divided into two equal parts, AND I
GIVE One equal half part thereof unto the direct
Heir Male of the Eldest Son of my Eldest Son,
in total exclusion of the younger Branches of my

Family and their descendants. AND as to the other equal half part of the said entire Principal Sum, I DIRECT my said Trustees to apply and dispose of the same in manner following (that is to say) IN the first place, in purchasing within the liberties of the City of London a plot of Freehold Ground of sufficient magnitude, and erecting thereon, under the superintendence of some eminent Architect, a Handsome and Substantial Building, with all suitable Offices, to be called "THE LONDON TREFALDEN BENEVOLENT INSTITUTION."

"'AND in the next place, in affording pecuniary aid as well permanent as temporary to decayed Tradesmen, Mercantile Men, Ship Brokers, Stock Brokers, Poor Clergymen, and Members of the Legal and Medical Professions, and the Widows and Orphans of each of those Classes respectively, and, if thought fit, to advance Loans without Interest to honest but unfortunate Bankrupts. With full power to receive into the Institution a limited number of poor and deserving Persons being Widows and Orphans of Citizens of London, and to maintain, clothe, and educate them so long as the Trustees shall think proper.

" ' AND in order that such Institution may be properly established and may be managed and supported in a satisfactory manner, I request my said Trustees to prepare a scheme for the permanent Establishment and support thereof, and to submit the same to the Master of the Rolls for his approval. PROVIDED ALWAYS that in case there shall be no such Male Heir in the direct line from the Eldest Son of my Eldest Son, Then I direct my said Trustees to apply the first mentioned half of the said entire principal sum in founding lesser Institutions of a similar kind to the above in Manchester, Liverpool, Bristol and Birmingham for the benefit of the several classes of persons above enumerated and all which Institutions it is my Will shall be governed by the same Laws and Regulations as the original Institution or as near thereto as circumstance will permit. ITEM I GIVE all the rest and residue of my Funded Property, Ready Money and Securities for Money, Merchandise, Debts, Pictures Plate, Furniture, and all other my Property not

otherwise disposed of by this my Will (but subject
to the payment of my Debts, Legacies, Funeral
and Testamentary expenses) UNTO my said three
Sons in equal shares and in case any dispute shall
arise between them as to the division thereof the
matter shall be referred to my Executors whose
decision shall be final. LASTLY I APPOINT
my friends Richard Morton, Erasmus Brooke,
Daniel Shuttleworth, and Arthur Mackenzie all
of London, General Merchants, to be the Executors of this my Will. IN WITNESS whereof I
the said Jacob Trefalden have hereunto set my
hand and seal the day and year first above
written.

" ' JACOB TREFALDEN.

" ' Signed sealed published and declared by the
above named Jacob Trefalden as and for his last
Will and Testament in the presence of us who at
his request and in his presence have subscribed
our Names as Witnesses thereunto.

" ' Signed.   " ' NATHANIEL MURRAY.
" ' ALEXANDER LLOYD.' "

Mr. Beavington laid down the will, and took

off his glasses. The brothers sat staring at him, like men of stone. William Trefalden was the first to speak.

"I shall dispute this will," he said, looking very pale, but speaking in a firm, low tone. "It is illegal."

"It is a damned, unnatural, infamous swindle," stammered Mr. Fred, starting from his seat, and shaking his clenched fist at the open document. "If I had known what a cursed old fool . . ."

"Hush, sir, hush, I entreat," interposed the lawyer. "Let us respect the dead."

"Zounds! Mr. Beavington, we'll respect the dead," said Captain Trefalden, bringing his hand down heavily upon the table; "but I'll be hanged if we'll respect the deed! If it costs me every penny of the paltry five thousand, I'll fight this matter out, and have justice."

"Patience, brother Jacob—patience, brother Fred," said the youngest Trefalden. "I tell you both, the will is illegal."

"How so, sir?" asked the lawyer, briskly. "How so?"

"By the Mortmain Act passed but a few years since . . ."

"In seventeen hundred and thirty-six, being the ninth of his present Majesty King George the Second," interposed Mr. Beavington.

"—which permits no money or land to be given in trust for the benefit of any charitable uses whatever."

The lawyer nodded approvingly.

"Very true, very true—very well remembered, Mr. Will," he said, rubbing his hands; "but you forget one thing."

"What do I forget?"

"That 'a citizen of London may, by the custom of London, devise Land situate in London in Mortmain; but he cannot devise Land out of the city in Mortmain,' and for that quotation I can give you chapter and verse, Mr. Will."

Mr. Will put his hand to his head with a smothered groan.

"Then, by Heavens!" said he, tremulously, "'tis all over."

It was all over, indeed. Mr. Fred had spoken truly of the pride which Jacob Trefalden took in his fortune. Great as it was, he resolved to build it yet higher, and sink its foundations yet more broadly and deeply. To leave a colossal inheritance to an unborn heir, and to found a charity which should perpetuate his name through all time, were the two projects nearest and dearest to that old man's heart. He had brooded over them, matured them, exulted in them secretly, for many a past year. The marriage of Captain Trefalden in November, 1759, only hastened matters, and legalised a foregone conclusion. Well was it for Jacob Trefalden's sons that his fortune amounted to that odd twenty-five thousand pounds. The Half Million had slipped through their fingers, and was lost to them for ever.

CHAPTER I.

WHEN the princess in the fairy tale went to sleep for a hundred years, everything else in that enchanted palace went to sleep at the same time. The natural course of things was suspended. Not a hair whitened on any head within those walls. Not a spider spun its web over the pictures; not a worm found its way to the books. The very Burgundy in the cellar grew none the riper for the century that it had lain there. Nothing decayed, in short, and nothing improved. Very different was it with this progressive England of ours during the hundred years that went by between the spring-time of 1760 and that of 1860, one hundred years after. None went to sleep in it. Nothing stood still. All was life, ferment, endeavour. That endeavour, it is true, may not

always have been best directed. Some cobwebs
were spun; some worms were at work; some
mistakes were committed; but, at all events,
there was no stagnation. *En revanche*, if, when
we remember some of those errors, we cannot
help a blush, our hearts beat when we think of
the works of love and charity, the triumphs of
science, the heroes and victories which that century brought forth. We lost America, it is true;
but we conquered India, we annexed the Canadas,
and we colonised New Zealand and Australia.
We fought the French on almost every sea and
shore upon the map, except, thank God! our
own. We abolished slavery in our colonies. We
established the liberty of the press. We lit our
great city from end to end with a light only
second to that of day. We invented the steam-
engine and the electric telegraph. We learned to
decipher those records which have been laid up
during countless ages in the heart of the everlast-
ing rocks. We discovered an unsuspected science
in the very speech we use. We originated a system
of coaching at twelve miles the hour, which was
unrivalled in Europe; and we superseded it by

casting a network of iron roads all over the face
of the country, along which the traveller has
been known to fly at the rate of a mile a minute.
Truly a marvellous century ! perhaps the most
marvellous which the world has ever known,
since that from which all our years are dated!

And during the whole of this time, the
Trefalden legacy was fattening at interest,
assuming overgrown proportions, doubling, trebl-
ing, quadrupling itself over and over and over
again.

Not so the Trefalden family. They had increased and multiplied but scantily, according to
the average of human kind; and had had but
little opportunity of fattening, in so far as that
term may be applied to the riches of the earth.
One branch of it had become extinct. Of the
other two branches only three representatives remained. We must pause to consider how these
things came to pass, but only for a few moments;
for of all the trees that have ever been cultivated
by man, the genealogical tree is the driest. It
is one, we may be sure, that had no place in the
garden of Eden. Its root is in the grave; its pro-

duce mere Dead Sea fruit—apples of dust and ashes.

The extinct branch of the Trefaldens was that which began and ended in Mr. Fred. That ornament to society met his death in a tavern row about eighteen months after the reading of the will. He had in the meanwhile spent the whole of his five thousand pounds, ruined his tailor, and brought an honest eating-house keeper to the verge of bankruptcy. He also died in debt to the amount of seven thousand pounds; so that, as Mr. Horace Walpole was heard to say, he at least went out of the world with credit.

William, the youngest of the brothers, after a cautious examination of his prospects from every point of view, decided to carry on at least a part of the business. To this end, he entered into partnership with his late father's managing clerk, an invaluable person who had been in old Jacob's confidence for more than thirty years, and, now that his employer was dead, was thought to know more about indigo than any other man in London. He had also a snug sum in the Funds, and an only daughter who kept house for him at Islington. When Mr. Will had ascertained the precise value of this young lady's attractions, he proposed a second partnership, was accepted, and married her. The fruit of this marriage was a son named Charles, born in 1770, who became in time his father's partner and successor, and in whose hands the old Trefalden house flourished bravely. This Charles, marrying late in life, took to wife the second daughter of a rich East India Director, with twelve thousand pounds for her fortune. She brought him four sons, the eldest of whom, Edward, born in 1815, was destined to indigo from his cradle. The second and third died in childhood, and the youngest, named William, after his grandfather, was born in 1822, and educated for the law.

The father of these young men died suddenly in 1844, just as old Jacob Trefalden had died more than eighty years before. He was succeeded in Basinghall-street by his eldest son. The new principal was, however, a stout, apathetic bachelor of self-indulgent habits, languid circulation, and indolent physique—a mere Roi Fainéant, without a Martel to guide him. He reigned only six years, and died of a flow of turtle soup to the head in 1850, leaving his affairs hopelessly involved, and his books a mere collection of Sibylline leaves which no accountant in London was Augur enough to decipher. With him expired the mercantile house of Trefalden; and his brother, the lawyer, now became the only remaining representative of the youngest branch of the family.

For the elder branch we must go back again to 1760.

Honest Captain Jacob, upon whom had now devolved the responsibility of perpetuating the Trefalden name, took his five thousand pounds with a sigh; wisely relinquished all thought of disputing the will; sold his commission; emigrated to a remote corner of Switzerland; bought land, and herds, and a quaint little mediæval chateau surmounted by a whole forest of turrets, gable-ends, and fantastic weather-cocks; and embraced the patriarchal life of his adopted country. Switzerland was at that time the most peaceful, the best governed, and the least expensive spot in Europe. Captain Jacob, with his five

thousand pounds, was a *millionnaire* in the Canton
Grisons.   He was entitled to a seat in the Diet,
if he chose to take it; and to a vote if he chose to
give it; and he interchanged solemn half-yearly
civilities with the stiffest old Republican aristo-
crats in Chur and Thusis.   But it was not for
these advantages that he valued his position in
that primitive place.   He loved ease, and liberty,
and the open air.   He loved the simple, pastoral,
homely life of the people.   He loved to be rich
enough to help his poorer neighbours—to be
able to give the pastor a new cassock, or the
church a new font, or the young riflemen of the
district a silver watch to shoot for, when the
annual *Schützen Fest* came round.   He could
not have done all this in England, heavily taxed
and burthened as England then was, upon two
hundred and fifty pounds a year.   So the good
soldier framed his commission, hung up his sword
to rust over the dining-room chimney-piece, and
planted and drained, sowed and reaped, shot an
occasional chamois, and settled down for life as a
Swiss country gentleman.   Living thus with the
wife of his choice, and enjoying the society of a

few kindly neighbours, he became the happy
father of a son and two daughters, between whom,
at his death, he divided his little fortune, share
and share alike, according to his own simple
notions of justice and love. The daughters married and settled far away, the one in Italy, the
other on the borders of Germany. The son, who
was called Henry, and born in 1762, inherited
his third of the patrimony, became a farmer, and
married at twenty years of age. He was neces-
sarily a much poorer man than his father. Two
thirds of the best land had been sold to pay off
his sisters' shares in the property; but he kept
the old château (though he dwelt in only a corner
of it), and was none the less respected by his
neighbours. Here he lived frugally and indus-
triously, often driving his own plough, and brand-
ing his own sheep; and here he brought up his
two sons, Saxon and Martin, the first of whom
was born in 1783, and the second in 1786. They
were all the family he reared. Other children
were born to him from time to time, and played
about his hearth, and gladdened the half-deserted
little château with their baby laughter; but they

all died in earliest infancy, and the violets grew thickly over their little graves in the churchyard on the hill.

Now Henry Trefalden knew right well that one of these boys, or a descendant of one of these boys, must inherit the great legacy by-and-by. He knew, too, that it was his duty to fit them for that gigantic trust as well as his poor means would allow, and he devoted himself to the task with a love and courage that never wearied. To make them honest, moderate, charitable, and self-denying; to teach them (theoretically) the true uses of wealth; to instruct them thoroughly in the history and laws of England; to bring them up, if possible, with English sympathies; to keep their English accent pure; to train them in the fear of God, the love of knowledge, and the desire of excellence—this was Henry Trefalden's life-long task, and he fulfilled it nobly.

His boys throve alike in body and in mind. They were both fine fellows; brave, simple, and true. Neither of them would have told a lie to save his life. Saxon was fair, as a Saxon should be. Martin was dark-eyed and olive-skinned like his mother. Saxon was the more active and athletic; Martin the more studious. As they grew older, Saxon became an expert mountaineer, rifle-shot, and chamois-hunter; Martin declared his wish to enter the Lutheran church. So the elder brother stayed at home, ploughing and planting, sowing and reaping, shooting and fishing, like his father and grandfather before him; and the younger trudged away one morning with his alpenstock in his hand and his wallet on his back, bound for Geneva.

Time went on. Henry Trefalden died; young Saxon became the head of the family; and Martin returned from the University to accept a curacy distant about eight miles from home. By-and-by, the good old priest who had been the boys' schoolmaster long years before, also passed away; and Martin became pastor in his native place. The brothers now lived with their mother in the dilapidated château, fulfilling each his little round of duties, and desiring nothing beyond them. They were very happy. That quiet valley was their world. Those Alps bounded all their desires. They knew there was a great legacy

accumulating in England, which might fall to
Saxon's share some day, if he lived long enough;
but the time was so far distant, and the whole
story seemed so dim and fabulous, that unless to
laugh over it together in the evening, when they
sat smoking their long pipes side by side under
the trellised vines, the brothers never thought or
spoke of the wealth which might yet be theirs.
Thus more time went on, and old Madame Trefalden died, and the bachelor brothers were left
alone in the little grey château.   It was now
1830.   In thirty more years the great legacy
would fall due, and which of them might then be
living to inherit it?   Saxon was already a florid
bald-headed mountaineer of forty-seven; Martin,
a grey-haired priest of forty-four.   What was to
be done?

Sitting by their own warm hearth one bleak
winter's evening, the two old bachelors took these
questions into grave consideration.   On the table
between them lay a faded parchment copy of the
alderman's last will and testament.   It was once
the property of worthy Captain Jacob, and had
remained in the family ever since.   They had

brought this out to aid their deliberations, and had read it through carefully, from beginning to end—without, perhaps, being very much the wiser.

"It would surely go to thee, Martin, if I died first," said the elder brother.

"Thou'lt not die first," replied the younger, confidently. "Thou'rt as young, Sax, as thou wert twenty years ago."

"But in the course of nature . . ."

"In the course of nature the stronger stuff outlasts the weaker. See how much heartier you are than myself?"

Saxon Trefalden shook his head.

"That's not the question," said he. "The real point is, *would* the money fall to thee? I think it would. It says here, '*in total exclusion of the younger branches of my family and their descendants.*' Mark that—'the younger branches,' Martin. Thou'rt not a younger branch. Thou'rt of the elder branch."

"Ay, brother, but what runs before? Go back a line, and thou 'lt see it says '*to the direct heir male of the eldest son of my eldest son.*' Now, thou 'rt the eldest son of the eldest son, and I am

not thy direct male heir. I am only thy younger
brother."

"That's true," replied Saxon. "It seems to
read both ways."

"All law matters seem to read both ways,
Sax," said the priest; "and are intended to read
both ways, 'tis my belief, for the confusion of the
world. But why puzzle ourselves about the will
at all? We can only understand the plain fact
that thou art the direct heir, and that the fortune
must be thine, thirty years hence, if thou 'rt alive
to claim it."

Saxon shrugged his broad shoulders, and lit
his pipe with a fragment of blazing pine wood
picked from the fire.

"Pish! at seventy-seven years of age, *if* I am
alive!" he exclaimed. "Of what good would it
be to me?"

Martin made no reply, and they were both
silent for several minutes. Then the pastor stole
a furtive glance at his brother, coughed, stared
steadily at the fire, and said :—

"There is but one course for it, Sax. Thou
must marry."

" Marry ! " echoed the stout farmer, all aghast.

The pastor nodded.

" Marry?   At my time of life?   At forty-
sev—— No, thank you, brother. Not if I
know it."

" Our poor father always desired it," said
Martin.

Saxon took no notice.

" And it is in some sense thy duty to provide
an heir to this fortune which . . ."

" The fortune be . . . I beg thy pardon,
Martin; but what can it matter to thee or
me what becomes of the fortune after we are
both dead and gone? It would go to found
charities, and do good somehow and somewhere.
'Twould be in better hands than mine, I 'll
engage."

" I am not so sure of that," replied the pastor.
" Public charities do not always do as much good
as private ones. Besides, I should like to think
that a portion of that great sum might be devoted
hereafter to the benefit of our poor brethren in
Switzerland. I should like to think that by-and-
by there might be a good road made between

Tamins and Flims; and that the poor herdsmen
at Altfelden might have a chapel of their own,
instead of toiling hither eight long miles every
Sabbath: and that a bridge might be built over
the Hinter Rhine down by Ortenstein, where
poor Rütli's children were drowned last winter
when crossing by the ferry."

Saxon smoked on in silence.

"All this might be done, and more," added the
pastor, "if thou wouldst marry, and bring up a
son to inherit the fortune."

"Humph !" ejaculated the farmer, looking
very grim.

"Besides," said Martin, timidly, "we want a
woman in the house."

"What for ?" growled Saxon.

"To keep us tidy and civilised," replied the
pastor. "Things were very different, Sax, when
our dear mother was with us. The house does
not look like the same place."

"There's old Lötsch," muttered Saxon. "He
does as well as any woman. He cooks, makes
bread . . ."

"Cooks ?" remonstrated the younger brother.

" Why, the kid to-day was nearly raw, and the mutton yesterday was baked to a cinder."

The honest farmer stroked his beard, and sighed. He could not contradict that stubborn statement. Martin saw his advantage, and followed it up.

" There is but one remedy," he said, "and that a plain one. As I told thee before, Sax, thou must marry. 'Tis thy duty."

" Whom can I marry?" faltered Saxon, dolefully.

" Well, I 've thought of that, too," rejoined the pastor, in an encouraging tone. " There's the eldest daughter of our neighbour Clauss. She is a good, prudent, housewifely maiden, and would suit thee exactly."

The elder brother made a wry face.

" She 's thirty-five, if she 's an hour," said he, " and no beauty."

" Brother Saxon," replied the pastor, "I am ashamed of thee. " What does a sensible man of seven-and-forty want with youth and beauty in a wife? Besides, Marie Clauss is only thirty-two.

I made particular inquiry about her age this morning."

"Why not marry her yourself, Martin?" said the farmer. "I'm sure that would do quite as well."

"My dear Saxon, only look again at the will, and observe that it is the direct heir male of the eldest son of the eldest son . . . ."

Saxon Trefalden pitched his pipe into the fire, and sprang to his feet with an exclamation that sounded very like an oath.

"Enough, brother, enough!" he interrupted. "Say no more—put the will away—I'll go down to the Bergthal to-morrow, and ask her."

And so Saxon Trefalden put on his Sunday coat the following morning, and went forth like a lamb to the sacrifice.

"Perhaps she'll refuse me," thought he, as he knocked at Farmer Clauss's door, and caught a glimpse of the fair Marie at an upper casement.

But that inexorable virgin did nothing of the kind.

She married him.

There were no ill-cooked dinners after that happy event had taken place. The old house became a marvel of cleanliness, and the bride proved herself a very Phœnix of prudence and housewifery.   She reformed everything — including the hapless brothers themselves.   She banished their pipes, condemned old Carlo to his kennel, made stringent by-laws on the subject of boots, changed the hour of every meal, and, in short, made them both miserable.   Worst of all, she was childless.   This was their bitterest disappointment.   They had given up their pipes, their peace, and their liberty, for nothing.   Poor Martin always looked very guilty if any allusion happened to be made to this subject.

Matters went on thus for seven years, and then, to the amazement of the village, and the delight of the brothers, Madame Marie made her husband the happy father of a fine boy.   Such a glorious baby was never seen !   He had fair hair and blue eyes, and his father's nose; and they christened him Saxon; and the bells were rung; and the heir to the great fortune was born at last !

CHAPTER II.

Two persons sat together in a first-floor room overlooking Chancery Lane. The afternoon sky was grey, and cold, and dull; and the room was greyer, colder, duller than the sky. Everything about the place looked sordid and neglected. The rain-channelled smoke of years had crusted on the windows. The deed-boxes on the shelves behind the door, the shabby books in the book-case opposite the fireplace, the yellow map that hung over the mantelpiece, the tape-tied papers on the table, were all thickly coated with white dust. There was nothing fresh or bright within those four walls, except a huge green safe with panelled iron doors and glittering scutcheons, fixed into a recess beside the fireplace. There were only two old-fashioned, horse-hair covered chairs in the room. There was not even a carpet on the floor. A more comfortless place could scarcely be conceived beyond the walls of a prison ; and yet, perhaps, it was not more comfortless than such places generally are.

It was the private room of William Trefalden, Esquire, attorney at law, and it opened out from the still drearier office in which his clerks were at work. There was a clock in each room, and an almanack on each mantelshelf. The hands of both clocks pointed to half-past four, and the almanacks both proclaimed that it was the second day of March, A.D. eighteen hundred and sixty.

The two persons sitting together in the inner chamber were the lawyer and one of his clients. Placed as he was with his back to the window and his face partly shaded by his hand, Mr. Trefalden's features were scarcely distinguishable in the gathering gloom of the afternoon. His client —a stout, pale man, with a forest of iron-grey hair about his massive temples—sat opposite, with the light full upon his face, and his hands crossed on the knob of his umbrella.

"I have come to talk to you, Mr. Trefalden," said he, "about that Castletowers mortgage."

"The Castletowers mortgage?" repeated Mr. Trefalden.

"Yes—I think I could do better with my money."

The lawyer shifted round a little farther from the light, and drew his hand a little lower over his eyes.

"What better do you think you could do with your money, Mr. Behrens?" he said, after a moment's pause. "It is an excellent investment. The Castletowers estate is burthened with no other incumbrance; and what can you desire better than five per cent. secured on landed property?"

"I have nothing to say against it, as an investment," replied the client; "but—I prefer something else."

Mr. Trefalden looked up with a keen, inquiring glance.

"You are too wise a man, I am sure, Mr. Behrens," said he, "to let yourself be tempted by any unsafe rate of interest."

The client smiled grimly.

"*You* are too wise a man, I should hope, Mr. Trefalden," rejoined he, "to suspect Oliver Behrens of any such folly? No, the fact is that five per cent. is no longer of such importance to me as it was seven years ago, and I have a mind to lay out that twenty-five thousand upon land."

"Upon land?" echoed the lawyer. "My dear sir, it would scarcely bring you three and a half per cent."

"I know that," replied the client. "I can afford it."

There was another brief silence.

"You will not give notice, I suppose," said Mr. Trefalden, quietly, "till you have seen something which you think likely to suit you."

"I have seen something already," replied Mr. Behrens.

"Indeed?"

"Yes; in Worcestershire—one hundred and thirty miles from London."

"Is that not somewhat far for a man of business, Mr. Behrens?"

"No, I have my box in Surrey, you know, adjoining the Castletowers grounds."

"True.   Have you taken any steps towards this purchase."

"I have given your address to the lawyers in whose care the papers are left, and have desired them to communicate with you upon the subject. I trust to you to see that the title is all as it should be."

Mr. Trefalden slightly bent his head.

"I will give you my best advice upon it," he replied.   "In the meantime, I presume, you would wish to give notice of your desire to call in your money."

"Precisely what I came here to do."

Mr. Trefalden took up a pen, and an oblong slip of paper.

"You will allow twelve months, of course?" said he, interrogatively.

"Certainly not.   Why should I?   Only six are stipulated for in the deed."

"True; but courtesy . . ."

"Tush! this is a matter of law, not courtesy," interrupted the client.

" Still, I fear it would prove a serious inconvenience to Lord Castletowers," remonstrated the lawyer. " Twenty-five thousand pounds is a large sum."

" Lord Castletowers' convenience is nothing to me," replied the other, abruptly. " I'm a man of the people, Mr. Trefalden. I have no respect for coronets."

" Very possible, Mr. Behrens," said Trefalden, in the same subdued tone; " but you may remember that your interest has been paid with scrupulous regularity, and that it is a very hard matter for a poor nobleman—Lord Castletowers *is* poor—to find so heavy a sum as twenty-five thousand pounds at only six months' notice."

" He did not think it too short when he gave me the bond," said Mr. Behrens.

" He wanted money," replied Mr. Trefalden, with a scarcely perceptible shrug of the shoulders.

" Well, and now *I* want it. Come, come, Mr. Trefalden, Lord Castletowers is your client, and no doubt you would like to oblige him; but I am your client too—and a better one than he is, I'll be bound ! "

"I trust, Mr. Behrens, that I should never seek to oblige one client at the expense of another," said the lawyer, stiffly. "If you think that I would, you wrong me greatly."

"I think, sir, that, like most other folks, you have more respect for a lord than a woolstapler," answered the man of the people, with a hard smile; "but I don't blame you for it. You're a professional man, and all professional men have those prejudices."

"I beg your pardon," said Mr. Trefalden. "I have none. I am the son of a merchant, and my family have all been merchants for generations. But this is idle. Let us proceed with our business. I am to take your instructions, Mr. Behrens, to serve Lord Castletowers with a notice of your determination to foreclose the mortgage in six months' time if your mortgage money is not repaid?"

Mr. Behrens nodded, and the lawyer made a note of the matter.

"I am also to understand that should Lord Castletowers request a further delay of six months you would not be disposed to grant it?"

" Certainly not."

Mr. Trefalden laid his pen aside.

"If he can't find the money," said the wool-stapler, "let him sell the old place. I'll buy it."

"Shall I tell his lordship so?" asked Mr. Trefalden, with a slight touch of sarcasm in his voice.

" If you like. But it won't come to that, Mr. Trefalden. You're a rich man—aha ! you needn't shake your head—you're a rich man, and you'll lend him the money."

" Indeed you are quite mistaken, Mr. Behrens," replied the lawyer, rising. " I am a very poor man."

" Ay, you say so, of course; but I know what the world thinks of your poverty, Mr. Trefalden. Well, good morning. You're looking pale, sir. You work too hard, and think too much. That's the way with you clever saving men. You should take care of yourself."

" Pshaw ! how can a bachelor take care of himself?" asked Mr. Trefalden, with a faint smile.

" True; you should look out for an heiress."

The lawyer shook his head.

E 2

LIBRARY
UNIVERSITY OF ILLINOIS

"No, no," said he, "I prefer my liberty. Good morning."

"Good morning."

Mr. Trefalden ushered his client through the office, listened for a moment to his heavy footfall going down the stairs, hastened back to his private room, and shut the door.

"Good God!" exclaimed he, in a low agitated tone, "what's to be done now? This is ruin— ruin!"

He took three or four restless turns about the room, then flung himself into his chair, and buried his face in his hands.

"He might well say that I looked pale," muttered he. "I felt pale. It came upon me like a thunderstroke. *I* a rich man, indeed! *I* with twenty-five thousand pounds at command! Merciful powers! what can I do? To whom can I turn for it? What security have I to give? Only six months' notice, too. I am lost! I am lost!"

He rose, and went to the great safe beside the fireplace. His hand trembled so that he could scarcely fit the key to the lock. He threw back one of the heavy iron-panelled doors, and brought

out a folded parchment, with the words " *Deed of*
MORTGAGE *between Gervase Leopold Wynnecliffe,*
Earl of Castletowers, and Oliver Behrens, Esq., of
Bread Street, London," written upon the outer
side.   Opening this document upon the desk, he
resumed his seat, and read it carefully through
from beginning to end.   As he did so, the trouble
deepened and deepened on his face, and his cheek
grew still more deathly.   When he came to the
signature at the end, he pushed it from him with
a bitter sigh.

"Not a flaw in it!" he groaned.   "No pretext
for putting off the evil day for even a week beyond
the time!   What a fool I was to think I could
ever replace it!   And yet what could I do?   I
wanted it.   If it were to do again to-morrow, I
should do it.   Yes, by Heaven! I should, be the
consequences what they might."

He paused, rose again, took a letter from the
table, and stood looking for some moments at the
signature.

"Oliver Behrens!" he mused.   "A bold hand,
with something of the German character in that
little twist at the top of the O——, a hand not

difficult to imitate, either! If, now, one only dared to frame an endorsement—but then there are the witnesses——No, no, impossible ! Better expatriation than such a risk as that. If the worst comes to the worst, there's always America."

And with this he sank down into his chair again, rested his chin upon his open palms, and fell into a deep and silent train of thought.

CHAPTER III.

As William Trefalden sat in his little dismal private room, wearily thinking, the clouds in the sky parted towards the west, and the last gleam of daylight fell upon his face. Such a pale eager face as it was, too, with a kind of strange beauty in it that no merely vulgar eye would have seen at all. To the majority of persons, William Trefalden was simply a gentlemanly "clever-looking" man. Attracted by the upright wall of forehead, which literally overbalanced the proportions of his face, they scarcely observed the delicacy of his other features. The clear pallor of his complexion, the subtle moulding of his mouth and chin, were altogether disregarded by those superficial observers. Even his eyes, large, brown, luminous as they were, lost much of their splendour

beneath that superincumbent weight of brow.
His age was thirty-eight; but he looked older.
His hair was thick and dark, and sprinkled lightly
here and there with silver. Though slender, he
was particularly well made—so well made, that it
seemed impossible to him to move ungracefully.
His hands were white and supple; his voice low;
his manner grave and polished. A very keen
and practised eye might, perhaps, have detected a
singular sub-current of nervous excitability beneath
that gravity and polish—a nervous excitability
which it had been the business of William Trefalden's whole life to conquer and conceal, and
which none of those around him were Lavaters
enough to discover. The ice of a studied reserve
had effectually crusted over that fire. His own
clerks, who saw him daily for three hundred and
thirteen dreary days in every dreary year, had no
more notion of their employer's inner life than
the veriest strangers who brushed past him along
the narrow footway of Chancery Lane. They saw
him only as others saw him. They thought of
him only as others thought of him. They knew
that he had a profound and extensive knowledge

of his profession, an iron will, and an inexhaustible reserve of energy. They knew that he would sit chained to his desk for twelve and fourteen hours at a time, when there was urgent business to be done. They knew that he wore a shabby coat, lunched every day on a couple of dry biscuits, made no friends, accepted no invitations, and kept his private address a dead secret, even from his head clerk. To them he was a grave, plodding, careful, clever man, somewhat parsimonious as to his expenditure, provokingly reticent as to his private habits, and evidently bent on the accumulation of riches. They were about as correct in their conclusions, as the conclave of cardinals which elected Pope Sixtus the Fifth for no other merits than his supposed age and infirmities.

Lost in anxious thought, William Trefalden sat at his desk in the same attitude till dusk came on, and the lamps were lighted in the thoroughfare below. Once or twice he sighed, or stirred uneasily; but his eyes never wandered from their fixed stare, and his head was never lifted from his hands. At length he seemed to come to a sudden resolution. He rose, rang the bell, crumpled up the memorandum which he had written according to Mr. Behrens' instructions, and flung it into the fire.

The door opened, and a red-headed clerk made his appearance.

"Let my office lamp be brought," said Mr. Trefalden, "and ask Mr. Keckwitch to step this way."

The clerk vanished, and was succeeded by Mr. Keckwitch, who came in with the lighted lamp in his hand.

"Put the shade over it, Keckwitch," exclaimed Mr. Trefalden, impatiently, as the glare fell full upon his face. "It's enough to blind one!"

The head clerk obeyed slowly, looking at his employer all the while from beneath his eye-lashes.

"You sent for me, sir?" he asked, huskily.

He was a short, fat, pallid man, with no more neck than a Schiedam bottle. His eyes were small and almost colourless. His ears had held so many generations of pens that they stood out from his head like the handles of a classic vase; and his voice was always husky.

" Yes. Do you know where to lay your hand upon that old copy of my great-grandfather's will?"

" Jacob Trefalden of Basinghall street, seventeen hundred and sixty ? "

Mr. Trefalden nodded.

The head clerk took the subject into placid consideration, and drummed thoughtfully with his fat fingers upon the most prominent portion of his waistcoat.

" Well, sir," he admitted, after a brief pause, " I won't say that I may not be able to find it."

" Do so, if you please. Who is in the office ? "

" Only Mr. Gorkin."

" Desire Gorkin to run out and fetch me a Continental Bradshaw."

Mr. Keckwitch retired; despatched the red-headed clerk; took down a bundle of dusty papers from a still dustier corner cupboard; brought forth the copy for which his employer had just inquired, and slipped the same within the lid of his desk. Having done this, he took another armful of mouldy papers from another shelf of the same cupboard, and littered them all about the desk and floor. Just as he had completed these arrangements, Gorkin returned, breathless, with the volume in his hand, and Mr. Keckwitch took it in.

" And the copy ? " said Mr. Trefalden, without lifting his eyes from an old book of maps over which he was bending.

" I am looking for it, sir," replied the head clerk.

" Very good."

" Gorkin may go, I suppose, sir ? It's more than half-past five."

" Of course; and you too, when you have found the deed."

Mr. Keckwitch retired again, released the grateful Gorkin, placed himself at his desk, and proceeded with much deliberation to read the will.

" What's at the bottom of it ? " muttered he, presently, as he paused with one fat finger on the opening sentence. " What's wrong? Something. I heard it in his voice. I saw it in his face. And he knew I should see it, too, when he called out about the shade. What is it ? What's he peering into those maps about ? Why

does he want this copy? He never asked for it
before. There ain't a farthing coming to him, I
know. I've read it before. But I'll read it
again, for all that. A man can never know too
much of his employer's private affairs. Not
much chance of learning a great deal of his,
either. Confounded private he keeps 'em."

He read on a little farther, and then paused
again.

"Why did he send for that Continental Bradshaw?" he questioned to himself. "Why can I
go, too, when there's plenty to be done here, and
he knows it? He wants me gone. Why? Where's
he goin' himself? What's he up to? Abel
Keckwitch, Abel Keckwitch, my best of friends,
keep your weather eye open!"

And with this apostrophe he returned to the
deed, and proceeded with it sedulously.

"Well, Keckwitch," cried Mr. Trefalden, from
the inner room, "have you found the copy?"

"Not yet, sir," replied the trusty fellow, who
was then rather more than half way through it.
"But I've turned out a boxful of old papers, and
I think I shall be sure . . ."

"Enough. Look closely for it, and bring it as soon as it turns up."

"It will turn up," murmured Mr. Keckwitch, "as soon as I have finished it."

And so it did, about five minutes after, when Mr. Keckwitch made his appearance with it at his master's door.

"Found? That's right!" exclaimed the lawyer, putting out his hand eagerly.

"I won't be sure, sir, till you've looked at it," replied the head clerk, with becoming modesty.

Mr. Trefalden's fingers closed on the parchment, but his eyes flashed keenly into the lustreless orbs of Mr. Abel Keckwitch, and rested there a moment before they reverted to the endorsement.

"Humph!" said he, in a slightly altered tone. "Yes—it's quite right, thank you. Good night."

"Good night, sir."

Mr. Trefalden looked after him suspiciously, and continued to do so, even when the door had been closed between them.

"The man's false," said he. "None but spies

have so little curiosity. I shouldn't wonder if
he has read every line."

Then he rose, locked the door, trimmed the
lamp, dismissed the subject from his thoughts,
and began to read the will. As he read, his
brow darkened, and his lip grew stern. Presently he pushed the deed aside, and jotted
down row after row of cyphers on a piece of
blotting-paper. Then he went back to the deed,
and back again to the cyphers, and every moment
the frown settled deeper and deeper on his brow.
Such a complex train of hopes and doubts, speculations and calculations as were traversing the
mazes of that busy brain! Sometimes he pondered in silence. Sometimes he muttered through
his teeth; but so inaudibly that had there even
been a listener at the door (as perhaps there was)
that listener would not have been a syllable the
wiser.

He took up a little almanack printed on a
card, and glanced at the number of days inter-
vening between the fourth and twenty-second of
March. There were just eighteen. Just eighteen
days to the expiration of this long, long century,

during which Jacob Trefalden's half million had
been accumulating, interest upon interest—during
which whole generations had been born, and lived,
and had passed away! Good Heavens! to what a
sum it had grown.   It amounted now to nine
million, five hundred and fifty-two thousand, four
hundred and odd pounds!   Words—mere words!
Words which no brain can distinctly realise.   He
might as well have tried to realise the distance
between the sun and the earth.   And this gigantic
bequest was to be divided between a charity and
an heir.   Half!   Even the half baffled him.
Even the half amounted to four million, seven
hundred and seventy-six thousand, two hundred
and odd pounds.   Pshaw! both sums were so
immense, that the one produced no more effect
upon his imagination than the other.

He took up his pen, and made a rapid calculation.   Supposing it were taken as an income at
five per cent.?   Ha! one could grasp that, at all
events.   It would produce about two hundred
and thirty-eight thousand pounds a year.   Two
hundred and thirty-eight thousand a year!   A
splendid revenue, truly; yet less than the income

enjoyed by many an English nobleman; and not one penny more than might be very easily and pleasantly spent by even a poor devil of an attorney like himself!

It might have been his own, that princely heritage—nay, would have been, but for the accursed accident of birth! It might have been his; and now to whom would it fall? To a stranger—an alien—probably to an uncultivated boor, ignorant of the very language of his forefathers! Oh, the bitter injustice of it! Had not *he* at least as fair a right to this wealth? Did not *he* stand in precisely the same degree of relationship to the giver of it? By what law of natural justice was the descendant of the eldest son to revel in superfluity, while he, the descendant of the youngest, stood on the brink of ruin? Had it even been left for division between the survivors, both might have been rich; but now——

He rose, pale and agitated, and paced restlessly about the room.

But now, was it not evident that this heir was his born foe and despoiler, and had he not the

right to hate him? Was not the hand of the
desperate man against all men, even from the
very beginning; but was it not first raised against
those who had wronged him the deepest?
William Trefalden was a desperate man. Had
he not appropriated that twenty-five thousand
pounds paid over to him by Lord Castletowers
two years ago for the liquidation of the mortgage, and did not ruin and discovery stare him in
the face? Having hazarded name and safety on
one terrible die known only to himself, should he
now hesitate to declare war upon his enemy, who
was the possessor of millions?

He smiled a strange smile of power and defiance,
and ran his finger along the black lines on the
map. From Dover to Calais—from Calais, by
train, to Basle—Basle to Zurich—Zurich to
Chur. At Chur the railways terminate. It
could not be far beyond Chur where these emi-
grant Trefaldens dwelt. It would take him three
days to get there, perhaps three and a half—
perhaps four. He would start to-morrow.

His decision once taken, William Trefalden
became in a moment cool and methodical as ever.

All trace of excitement vanished from his face, as a breath clears from the surface of a mirror. He thrust the Bradshaw in his pocket, scribbled a hasty note to his head clerk, carefully burned the cyphered blotting-paper in the flame of the candle, and watched it expire among the dead ashes in the fireplace; locked his desk; tried the fastenings of the safe; glanced at the clock, and prepared to be gone.

"A quarter to seven already!" exclaimed he, as he unlocked the door. "I shall be late to-night!"

He had spoken aloud, believing himself alone, but stopped at the sight of Mr. Keckwitch, busily writing.

"You here, Keckwitch!" he said, frowning. "I told you you might go."

"You did, sir," replied the scribe, placidly; "but there was Heywood and Bennett's deed of partnership to be drawn up, so I would not take advantage of your kindness."

Trefalden bit his lip.

"I had just written a line to you," he said, "to let you know that I am going out of town for a fortnight. Forward all letters marked private."

" Where to, sir ? "

" You will find the address here."

And Mr. Trefalden tossed the note down upon the clerk's desk, and turned towards the door.

" Glad you're going to allow yourself a little pleasure for once, sir," observed Mr. Keckwitch, without the faintest gleam of surprise or curiosity on his impassive countenance. " Begging pardon for the liberty."

His employer hesitated for an instant before replying.

" Thank you," he said, " but pleasure is not my object. I go to visit a relation whom I have neglected too long. Good night."

With this he passed from the room, and went slowly down the stairs. In the passage he paused to listen; and when in the street, stepped out into the middle of the thoroughfare to look up at the windows.

"Strange ! " muttered he ; " but I never suspected that fellow so strongly as I do to-night ! "

He then glanced right and left, buttoned his coat across his chest, for the March wind blew keenly, and walked briskly up the lane, in the direction of Holborn. As he neared the top of the street, close to its junction with the great thoroughfare, a thought struck him, and he flung himself back, by a rapid movement, into the recess of an old-fashioned doorway. There was no lamp within several yards. The doorway was dark and deep as a sentry box. There, with eager ear and bated breath, he waited.

Presently, apart from the deep hum of traffic close by, he heard a footstep coming up—a footstep so light and swift that at first he thought he must be mistaken. Then his practised ear detected a labouring wheeze in the breath of the runner.

"The scoundrel!" ejaculated he, poised his right arm, set his teeth, and stood ready for a spring.

The signals of distress grew more distinct. The step slackened—ceased—drew near again—and Mr. Abel Keckwitch, panting and bewildered, made his appearance just opposite the doorway,

evidently baffled by the disappearance of its
occupant.

He was not long left in doubt. Swift as a
panther, William Trefalden swooped down upon
his man, and dealt him a short powerful blow that
sent him reeling, pale and giddy, against the wall.
It was surprising what muscles of steel and
knuckles of iron lay *perdu* beneath the white
superficies of that supple hand.

"Dog!" said he, fiercely, "do you dare to spy
at my heels? This is not the first time I've
suspected you; but I advise you to let it be the
last time I convict you. Ay, you may scowl, but,
by the Heaven above me! if I catch you at this
game again, you'll repent it to your dying day.
There! be thankful that I let you off so cheaply."

And having said this, William Trefalden walked
coolly away without vouchsafing so much as a
glance to a couple of delighted boys who stood
watching the performance from the opposite side
of the street.

As for Abel Keckwitch, he recovered his breath
and his equilibrium as well as he could, though
the former was a matter of time, and caused him

to sit down, ignominiously, on the nearest door-step. When, at length, he was in a condition to retrace his steps, he rose, shook his fat fist in a passion of impotent rage, and indulged in a volley of curses, not loud but deep.

"I'll be even with you," gasped he, more huskily than ever. "I'll be even with you, Mr. Trefalden, if I die for it! You've something to hide, but you shan't hide it from me. I'll know where you live, and what you do with your money. I'll find out the secret of your life before I've done with you, and then let us see which will be master!"

CHAPTER IV.

Amid the many hundred miles which it traverses from its source in the glacier-land to its dispersion among the border flats of the Zuyder Zee, the great Rhine river flows through no district so full of strange interest, so wild, so primitive, so untrodden, as that deep and lonely valley that lies between Chur and Thusis in the Canton Grisons. The passing traveller hastening on to the Splugen, the wandering artist eager for Italy, alike hurry past with scarce a glance or a thought for the grey peaks above, or the stony river-bed below the beaten highway. They little guess what green delicious valleys, what winding ravines, what legend-haunted ruins, and fragrant uplands jewelled with Alp-roses and purple gentian blossoms, lie all unsought among the slopes

and passes of the mountains round about. Still-
less do they dream that to some of those crumb-
ling towers from which the very ivy has long
since withered away, there cling traditions many
centuries older than Christ; or that in yonder scattered châlets, some of which cluster like swallows'
nests on shelves of granite six or eight hundred
feet above the level of the valley, there is yet
spoken a language unknown to the rest of Europe.
Only the historian and archæologist care to remember how there lie embedded in that tongue
the last fragments of a forgotten language; and
how in the veins of the simple mountaineers who
speak it, there yet linger some drops of the blood
of a lost, a mighty, and a mysterious people.

Thus it happened that William Trefalden, who
was neither an archæologist nor an historian, but
only a brilliant, unscrupulous man of the world,
every fibre of whose active brain was busy just
then with a thousand projects, neither knew, nor
cared to know any of these things; but took his
way up the valley of Domleschg without bestowing
a thought upon its people or traditions.

It was about three o'clock in the afternoon of

the fourth day from that on which he left London. He had been on the road two nights out of the three ; and yet his eye looked none the less bright, and his cheek none the paler. As he strode along in the deep shade, glancing up from time to time at the sunny heights above his head, his step grew freer, and his bearing more assured than usual. There was not a soil of travel on his garments. The shabby office coat so inseparably associated with its wearer in the minds of his clerks, was discarded for a suit of fashionable cut and indefinite hue, such as the British tourist delighteth to honour. His gloves and linen were faultless. Even his boots, although he was on foot, were almost free from dust. He looked, in short, so well dressed, and so unlike his daily self, that it may be doubted whether even Mr. Abel Keckwitch would have recognised his employer at the first glance, if that astute head-clerk could by any possibility have met him on the way.

Absorbed in thought as he was, however, Mr. Trefalden paused every now and then to reconnoitre the principal features of the valley, and

make certain of his landmarks. The village
from which he had started was already left two
miles behind; and, save a ruined watch-tower on
a pedestal of rock some eighty feet above the
level of the road, there was no accessible building
in sight. The Hinter Rhine, with its grey waters
still dull from the glacier, ran brawling past him
all the way. There were pine forests climbing
up the spurs of the mountains; and flocks of
brown goats, with little tinkling bells about
their necks, browsing over the slopes lower
down. Far above the sound of these little bells,
uplifted, as it were, upon gigantic precipices
of bare granite, rose, terrace beyond terrace, a
whole upper world of pasture lands, cultivated
fields, mossy orchards, and tiny hamlets, which,
seen from the valley, looked like carved toys
scattered over the sward. Higher still came
barren plateaus, groups of stunted firs, and
rugged crags, still thickly sheeted with snow;
while far away to the right, where another
valley seemed to open westward, rose a mountain
loftier than all the rest, from the summit of
which a vast glacier hung over in icy folds that

glittered to the sun, like sculptured drapery depending from the shoulder of some colossal statue.

But William Trefalden had no eyes for this grand scene. To him, at that moment, the mountains were but sign-posts, and the sun a lamp to light him on his way. He was seeking for a certain roadside shrine behind which, he had been told, he should find a path leading to the Château Rotzberg. He knew that he had not yet passed the shrine, and that by this time he must be near it. Presently a chapel-bell chimed from the heights, clear, and sweet, and very distant. He paused to glance at his watch, and then pressed forward more rapidly. It was already a quarter to three, and he was anxious to reach his destination before the afternoon should grow much later. There was an abrupt curve in the road a few yards further on. He had been looking forward to this point for some minutes, and felt so sure that it must bring him in sight of the path, that when it actually did so, he struck up at once through the scattered pines that fringed the waste ground to the left of the road, and trod the beaten

track, as confidently as if he were familiar with
every foot of the way.

As he went on, the sound of the hurrying river
died away, and the scattered pines became a thick
plantation, fragrant and dusky. Then the ground
grew hilly, and was broken up here and there by
mossy boulders; and then came open daylight
again, and a space of smooth sward, and a steep
pathway leading up to another belt of pines.
This second plantation was so precipitous that the
path had in some places been laid down with
blocks of rough stone, and short lengths of pine
trunks, so as to form a kind of primitive stair-
case up the mountain-side. The ascent, however,
was short, though steep, and Mr. Trefalden had
not been climbing it for many minutes before he
saw a bright shaft of sunlight piercing the fringed
boughs some few yards in advance. Then the moss
became suddenly golden beneath his feet, and he
found himself on the verge of an open plateau,
with the valley lying in deep shade some four
hundred feet below. There ran the steel-grey
river, eddying but inaudible; there opened the
broad Rheinthal, leading away mile after mile into

the dim distance, with glimpses of white Alps on the horizon; while close by, within fifty yards of the spot on which he was standing, rose the ivied walls of the Château Rotzberg.

This, then, was the home to which his great-grandfather's eldest son had emigrated one hundred years before—this, the birthplace of the heir at law! William Trefalden smiled somewhat bitterly as he paused and looked upon it.

It was a thorough Swiss, mediæval dwelling, utterly irregular, and consisting apparently of a cluster of some five or six square turrets, no two of which were of the same size or height. They were surmounted alike by steep slated roofs and grotesque weathercocks; and the largest, which had been suffered to fall to ruin, was green with ivy from top to bottom. The rest of the château gave signs of only partial habitation. Many of the narrow windows were boarded up, while others showed a scrap of chintz on the inner side, or a flower-pot on the sill. A low wall enclosing a small courtyard lay to the south of the building, and was approached by a quaint old gateway supporting a sculptured scutcheon, close above which a stork had built his nest.

None of these details escaped the practised eye of William Trefalden. He saw all in a moment —poverty, picturesqueness, and neglect. As he crossed the open sward, and came in sight of a steep road winding up from the valley on the other side, he remarked that there were no tracks of wheels upon it. Passing under the gateway, he observed how the heraldic bearings were effaced upon the shield, and how those fractures were such as could only have been dealt by the hand of man. Not even the grass that had sprung up amid the paving in the courtyard, nor the mossy penthouse over the well, nor the empty kennel in the corner, remained unnoticed as he went up to the door of the château.

It was standing partly open—a massy oaken portal, studded with iron stanchions, and protected only by a heavy latch. William Trefalden looked round for a bell, but there was none. Then he knocked with his clenched hand, but no one came. He called aloud, but no one answered. At last he went in.

The door opened into a stone hall of irregular shape, with a cavernous fireplace at one end, and a large modern window at the other. The ceiling was low, and the rafters were black with smoke. An old carved press, a screen, some chairs and settles of antique form, a great oak table on which lay a newspaper and a pair of clumsy silver spectacles, a curious Swiss clock with a toy skeleton standing in a little sentry-box just over the dial, a spinning-wheel and a linen-press, were all the furniture that it contained. A couple of heavy Tyrolean rifles, with curved stocks to fit to the shoulder, were standing behind the door, and an old sabre, a pair of antlers, and a yellow parchment in a black frame, hung over the mantelpiece. A second door, also partly open, stood nearly opposite the first, and led into a garden.

Having surveyed this modest interior from the threshold, and found himself alone there, Mr. Trefalden crossed over to the fireplace and examined the parchment at his leisure. It was Captain Jacob's commission, signed and sealed by His Most Gracious Majesty King George the Second, Anno Domini seventeen hundred and forty-eight. Turning from this to the newspaper on the table, he saw that it was printed in some language with which he was not acquainted—a language that was neither French, nor Italian, nor Spanish, but which seemed to bear a vague resemblance to all three. It was entitled "*Amity del Pievel.*" Having lingered over this journal with some curiosity, he laid it down again, and passed out through the second door into the garden.

Here, at least, he had expected to find some one belonging to the place; but it was a mere kitchen garden, and contained nothing higher in the scale of creation than cabbages and potatoes, gooseberry bushes and beds of early salad. Mr. Trefalden began to ask himself whether his Swiss kindred had deserted the Château Rotzberg altogether.

Strolling slowly along a side path sheltered by a high privet hedge, and glancing back every now and then at the queer little turretted building with all its weathercocks glittering in the sun, he suddenly became aware of voices not far distant. He stopped—listened—went on a few steps farther—and found that they proceeded from some lower level than that on which he stood. Having once ascertained the direction of the sounds, he followed them rapidly enough. His quick eye detected a gap in the hedge at the upper end of the garden. From this gap, a flight of rough steps led down to a little orchard some eighteen or twenty feet below—a mere shelf of verdure on the face of the precipice, commanding a glorious view all over the valley, and lying full to the sunset. It was planted thickly with fruit trees, and protected at the verge of the cliff by a fragile rail. At the farther end, built up in an angle of the rock, stood a rustic summer-house newly thatched with Indian corn-straw. Towards this point William Trefalden made his way through the scant grass, in which as yet no wildflowers were to be seen.

As he drew nearer, he heard the sounds again. There was but one voice now—a man's—and he was reading. What was he reading? Not German. Not that strange dialect printed in the "*Amity del Pievel.*" Certainly not Latin. He advanced a little farther. Was it, could it be —Greek?

Mr. Trefalden's Greek had grown somewhat rusty these last eighteen years or so; but there could be no mistake about those sonorous periods. He recognised the very lines as they fell from the lips of the speaker—lines sweet and strong as that god-like wine stored of old in the chamber of Ulysses. It was many and many a year since he had heard them, though at Eton they had been "familiar in his mouth as household words:"

> About our heads elms and tall poplars whispered ;
> While from its rocky cave beside us trickled
> The sacred waters of a limpid fountain.
> The cricket chirped i' the hedge, and the sweet throstle
> Sang loudly from the copse.

Who should this be but Theocritus of Sicily? William Trefalden could scarcely believe his ears. Theocritus in the valley of Domleschg! Theocritus in the mouths of such outer barbarians as the dwellers in the Château Rotzberg?

Having ended the famous description of the garden of Phrasidamus, the reader paused. William Trefalden hastened up to the front of the summer-house. An old man smoking a German pipe, and a youth bending over a book, were its only occupants. Both looked up, and both, by a simultaneous impulse of courtesy, rose to receive him.

"I beg your pardon," he said, lifting his hat. "This is, I fear, an unceremonious intrusion; but I am not quite a stranger, and . . ."

He checked himself. French was the language which he had found generally understood in the Grisons, and he had inadvertently used his native English.

But the old man bowed, laid his pipe aside, and replied in English as pure as his own.

"Whoever you may be, sir, you are welcome."

"I think I have the pleasure of addressing a relative," observed the lawyer. "My name is William Trefalden."

The old man stepped forward, took him by both hands, and, somewhat to his surprise, kissed him on each cheek.

"Cousin," he said, "thou art thrice welcome. Saxon, my son, embrace thy kinsman."

CHAPTER V.

MR. TREFALDEN took the rustic chair handed to him by his younger kinsman, and placed it just against the entrance to the summer-house. It was his habit, he said, to avoid a strong light, and the sunset dazzled him. The old man resumed his seat. The youth remained standing. Both looked at the new comer with a cordial, undissembled curiosity; and for a few seconds there was silence.

Mr. Trefalden's elder kinsman was fragile, pale, white-haired, with brilliant dark eyes, and thin sensitive lips, that trembled when he spoke earnestly. The other was a tall, broad-shouldered, broad-browed, powerful young fellow, with a boyish down upon his upper lip, and a forest of

thick golden-brown hair, crisp and curly as the
locks of Chaucer's Squire. His eyebrows and
eyelashes were some shades darker than his
hair; and his eyes looked out from beneath them
with an expression half shy, half fearless, such as
we sometimes see in the eyes of children. In
short, he was as goodly a specimen of the race
of Adam as one might hope to meet with between
London and the valley of Domleschg, or even
farther; and this Mr. Trefalden could not but
admit at the first glance.

The old man was the first to speak.

"You did not find your way without a guide,
cousin?" said he.

"It was no very difficult achievement," replied
the lawyer. "I enjoyed the walk."

"From Chur?"

"No—from Reichenau. I have taken up my
quarters at the 'Adler.' My landlord described
the road to me. It was easy enough to find;
not, perhaps, quite so easy to follow."

"Ah, you came by the footpath. It is sadly
out of repair, and would seem steep to a stranger. Saxon, go bid Kettli prepare supper; and

open a bottle of d'Asti wine. Our cousin is weary."

Mr. Trefalden hastened to excuse himself; but it was of no avail. The old gentleman insisted that he should "at least break bread and drink wine" with them; and Mr. Trefalden, seeing that he attached some patriarchal import to this ceremony, yielded the point.

"You have a son, sir, of whom you may be proud," said he, looking after the youth as he strode away through the trees.

The old man smiled, and with the smile his whole face grew tender and gracious.

"He is my great hope and joy," he replied; "but he is not my son. He is the only child of my dear brother, who died twelve years ago."

Mr. Trefalden had already heard this down at Reichenau, but he said, "Indeed?" and looked interested.

"My brother was a farmer," continued the other; "I entered the Lutheran church. He married late in life; I have been a bachelor all my days."

"And your brother's wife," said Mr. Trefalden, "is she still living?"

"No; she died two years after she became a mother. For twelve years, Saxon has had no parent but myself. He calls me 'father'—I call him 'son.' I could not love him more if he were really my own offspring. I have been his only tutor, also. I have taught him all that I know. Every thought of his heart is open to me. He is what God and my teaching have made him."

"He is a magnificent fellow, at all events," said Mr. Trefalden, drily.

"My brother was almost as tall and handsome at his age," replied the pastor, with a sigh.

"What *is* his age?" asked the lawyer.

"He was twenty-two on the thirtieth of last December."

"I should not have taken him to be more than twenty."

"Twenty-two — twenty-two years, and four months—a man in age, in stature, in strength, in learning; but a boy at heart, cousin—a boy at heart!"

"All the better for him," said Mr. Trefalden,

with his quiet voice, and pleasant smile. "Many of the greatest men that ever lived were boys to the last."

"I have no desire to see my Saxon become a great man," said Martin Trefalden, hastily. "God forbid it! I have tried to make him a good man. That is enough."

"And I have no doubt that you have succeeded."

The old man looked troubled.

"I have tried," said he; "but I know not whether I have tried in the right way. I have trained him according to my own belief, and ideas; and what I have done has been done for the best. I may have acted wrongly. I may not have done my duty; but I have striven to do it. I prayed for light—I prayed for God's blessing on my work. I believed my prayers were heard; but I have had heavy misgivings of late —heavy, heavy misgivings!"

"I feel sure they must be groundless," said Mr. Trefalden.

The pastor shook his head. He was evidently anxious, and ill at ease.

"That is because you do not know," replied
he. "I cannot tell you now—another time—
when we can be longer alone. In the meanwhile,
I thank Heaven for the chance that has brought
you hither. Cousin, you are our only surviving
kinsman—you are acquainted with the world—
you will advise me—you will be good to him! I
am sure you will. I see it in your face."

"I shall be very glad to receive your confidence,
and to give you what counsel I can," replied Mr.
Trefalden.

"God bless you!" said the pastor, and shook
hands with him across the table.

At this moment there came a sound of voices
from the farther end of the terrace.

"One word more," cried Martin, eagerly.
"You know our family history, and the date that
is drawing near?"

"I do."

"Not a syllable before *him*, till we have again
spoken together. Hush! he is here."

A giant shadow fell upon the grass, and young
Saxon's six feet of substance stood between them
and the sun. He held a dish in his hands and a

bottle under his arm, and was followed by a
stalwart peasant woman, laden with plates and
glasses.

"The evening is so mild," said he, "that I
thought our cousin would prefer to stay here;
so Kettli and I have brought the supper with us."

"Nothing could please me better," replied
Mr. Trefalden. "By the way, Saxon, I must
compliment you on your Greek. Theocritus is
an old friend of mine, and you read him remarkably well."

The young man, who had just removed the
book from the table, and was assisting to spread
the cloth, blushed like a girl.

"He and Anacreon were my favourite poets,"
added the lawyer; "but that was a long time
ago. I fear I now remember very little of
either."

"I have not read Anacreon," said Saxon; "but
of all those I know, I love Homer best."

"Ay, for the fighting," suggested his uncle,
with a smile.

"Why not, when it's such grand fighting?"

"Then you prefer the Iliad to the Odyssey,"

said Mr. Trefalden. "Now, for my part, I always took more pleasure in the adventures of Ulysses. The scenery is so various and romantic; the fiction so delightful."

"I don't like Ulysses," said Saxon, bluntly. "He's so crafty."

"He is therefore all the truer to nature," replied Mr. Trefalden. "All Greeks are crafty; and Ulysses is the very type of his race."

"I cannot forgive him on that plea. A hero must be better than his race, or he is no hero at all."

"That is true, my son," said the pastor.

"I allow that the Homeric heroes are not Bayards; but they are great men," said Mr. Trefalden, defending his position less for the sake of argument than for the opportunity of studying his cousin's opinions.

"Ulysses is not a great man," replied Saxon, warmly; "much less a hero."

Mr. Trefalden smiled, and shook his head.

"You have all the world against you," said he.

"The world lets itself be blinded by tradition," answered Saxon. "Can a man be a hero, and steal? a hero, and tell lies? a hero, and afraid to give his name? Tell of Altdorf was not one of that stamp. When Gessler questioned him about the second arrow, he told the truth, and was ready to die for it."

"You are an enthusiast on the subject of heroes," said Mr. Trefalden, jestingly.

The young man blushed again, more deeply than before.

"I hate Ulysses," he said. "He was a contemptible fellow; and I don't believe that Homer wrote the Odyssey at all."

With this he addressed some observation to Kettli, who answered him, and took her departure.

"What a strange dialect!" said Mr. Trefalden, his attention diverted into another channel. "Did I not see a newspaper printed in it, as I passed just now through the house?"

"You did; but it is no dialect," replied the pastor, as they took their places round the table. "It is a language—a genuine language; copious, majestic, elegant, and more ancient by many centuries than the Latin."

"You surprise me."

"Its modern name," continued the old man, "is the Rhæto-Romansch. If you desire to know its ancient name, I must refer you back to a period earlier, perhaps, than even the foundation of Alba Longa, and certainly long anterior to Rome. But, cousin, you do not eat."

"I have really no appetite," pleaded Mr. Trefalden, who found neither the goat's-milk cheese nor the salad particularly to his taste. "Besides, I am much interested in what you tell you."

The pastor's face lighted up.

"I am glad of it," he said, eagerly. "I am very glad of it. It is a subject to which I have devoted the leisure of a long life."

"But you have not yet told me the ancient name of this Romansch tongue?"

Saxon, who had been looking somewhat uneasy during the last few minutes, was about to speak; but his uncle interposed.

"No, no, my son," he said, eagerly, "these are matters with which I am more conversant than thou. Leave the explanation to me."

The young man bent forward, and whispered, "Briefly, then, dearest father."

Mr. Trefalden's quick ear caught the almost inaudible warning. It was his destiny to gain more than one insight into character that evening.

The pastor nodded somewhat impatiently, and launched into what was evidently a favourite topic.

"Look round," he said, "at these mountains. They have their local names, as the Galanda, the Ringel, the Albula, and so forth; but they have also a general and classified name. They are the Rhætian Alps. Among them lie numerous valleys, of which this, the Hinter-Rhein-Thal, is the chief. Yonder lie the passes of the Splugen and the Stelvio, and beyond them the plains of Lombardy. You probably know this already; but it is important to my explanation that you should have a correct idea of our geography here in the Grisons."

Mr. Trefalden bowed, and begged him to proceed. Saxon ate his supper in silence.

"Well," continued the pastor, "about two thou-

sand eight hundred years ago, these Alps were
peopled by a hardy aboriginal race, speaking the
same language, or the germs of the same language, which is spoken here to this day by their
descendants. These aborigines followed the in-
stincts which God would seem to have implanted
in the hearts of all mountain races. They wearied of their barren fastnesses. They poured
down into the southern plains. They expelled
the native Umbrians, and settled as conquerors
in that part of Italy which lies north of Ancona
and the Tiber. There they built cities, cultivated
literature and the arts, and reached a high degree
of civilization. When I tell you that they had
attained to this eminence before the era of
Romulus ; that they gave religion, language, and
arts to Rome herself; that, according to the
decreed fate of nations, they fell through their
own luxury and were enslaved in their turn ;
that, pursued by the Gaul or the Celt, they fled
back at last to these same mountains from which
they had emigrated long centuries before ; that
they erected some of those strongholds, the im-
perishable ruins of which yet stand above our

passes; and that in this Rhæto-Romansch tongue
of the Grisons survive the last utterances of their
lost poets and historians—when, cousin, I tell
you all these things, you will, I think, have
guessed already what the name of that ancient
people must have been?"

Now it happened, somewhat unluckily, that
Mr. Trefalden had lately read, somewhere or another, a review of somebody's book on this very
subject; so, when the old man paused, quite
warm and flushed with his own eloquence, he
found himself prepared with a reply.

" If," said he, " I had not taken an impression—if, in short, I had had not understood
that the Etruscans were originally a Lydian
tribe . . ."

" You took that impression from Herodotus! "
interrupted the pastor.

" Not to my knowledge."

" From Tacitus, then ?"

" Possibly from Tacitus."

" Yes, Tacitus supports that theory, but he is
wrong; so does Herodotus, and he is wrong; so
do Strabo, Cicero, Seneca, Pliny, Plutarch,

Velleius Paterculus, Servius, and a host of others, and they are all wrong—utterly wrong, every one of them!"

"But where . . ."

"Livy supposes that the emigration was from the plains to the mountains—folly, mere folly! Does not every example in history point to the contrary? The dwellers in plains fly to the mountains for refuge; but emigration flows as naturally from the heights to the flats, as streams flow down from the glaciers to the valleys. Hellanicus of Lesbos would have us believe they were Pelasgians. Dionysius of Halicarnassus asserts that they were the aborigines of the soil. Gorius makes them Phœnician—Bonarota, Egyptian—Maffei, Canaanite—Guarnacci . . ."

"I beg your pardon," interrupted Mr. Trefalden; "but when I said I had understood that the Etruscans were of Lydian origin . . ."

"They were nothing of the kind!" cried the pastor, trembling with excitement. "If they had been his countrymen, would not Xantus of Lydia have chronicled the event? He never even names them. Can you conceive an English historian omit-

ting the colonisation of America; or a Spanish historian passing over the conquest of Mexico? No,
cousin, you must forgive me for saying that he
who embraces the empty theories of Herodotus
and Tacitus commits a grievous error; and I can
show you such archæological evidence . . ."

"I assure you," said Mr. Trefalden, laughingly,
"that I have not the least disposition to do anything of the kind. It is a subject upon which I
know absolutely nothing."

"And, father," began Saxon, laying his hand
gently on the old man's arm, "I think you
forget . . ."

"No, no, I forget nothing," interrupted his
uncle, too much possessed by his own argument
to listen to any one. "I do not forget that
Gibbon pronounced the Lydian theory a theme
for only poets and romancists. I do not forget
that Steub, whatever the tenor of his other
opinions, at least admitted the unity of the
Etruscan and Rhætian tongues. Then there was
Niebuhr—although *he* fell under the mistake of
supposing the Etruscan to be a mixed race, he
believed the Rhætians of these Alps to have been

the true stock, and maintained that they reduced
the Pelasgi to a state of vassalage.   Niebuhr was
a great man, a fine historian, an enlightened
scholar.   I corresponded with him, cousin, for
years, on this very subject; but I could never
succeed in convincing him of the purely Rhætian
nationality of the Etruscan people.   He always
would have it that they were amalgamated with
the Pelasgians.   It was a great pity !   I wish I
could have set him right before he died."

Mr. Trefalden looked at his watch.

"I wish you could," he said; "but it grows
late, and I shall never find my way back before
dark, if I do not at once bid you good evening."

The pastor put his hand to his brow in a bewildered way.

"I—I fear I have talked too much," he said,
shyly.   "I have wearied you.   Pray forgive me.
When I begin upon this subject, I do not know
where to stop."

"That is because you know so much about it,"
replied the lawyer.   "But I have listened with
great pleasure, I assure you."

"Have you ?   Have you, indeed ? "

" And have learned a great deal that I did not know before."

" I will show you all Niebuhr's letters, another time, and copies of my replies," said the old man, " if you care to read them."

He was now quite radiant again, and wanted only a word of encouragement to resume the conversation; but Mr. Trefalden had had more than enough of the Etruscans already.

"Thank you," said he; "thank you—another time.   And now, good-bye."

"No, no—stay a moment longer.   I have so much to say to you—so many questions to ask. How long do you stay in Reichenau?"

" Some days—perhaps a week."

" Are you on your way to Italy?"

" Not at all.   I wanted change of air, and I have come abroad for a fortnight's holiday.   My object in choosing Reichenau for a resting-place, is solely to be near you."

The old man's eyes filled with tears.

"How good of you!" he said simply.   "I should never have seen you if you had not found your way hither—and, after all, we three are

the last of our name. Cousin, will you come
here ? "

Mr. Trefalden hesitated.

"What do you mean?" he said. "I shall
come again, of course, to-morrow."

"I mean, will you come here for the time of
your stay? I hardly like to ask you, for I know
the 'Adler' is far more comfortable than our
little desolate eyrie. But still, if you can put up
with farmer's fare and mountain habits, you shall
have a loving welcome."

Mr. Trefalden smiled, and shook his head.

"I thank you," said he, "as much as if I
accepted your hospitality; but it is impossible.
We Londoners lead busy feverish lives, and
become enslaved by all kinds of unhealthy customs. Your habits and mine differ as widely as
the habits of an Esquimaux and a Friendly
Islander. Shall I confess the truth? You have
just supped—I am now going back to Reichenau
to dinner."

" To dinner ? "

" Yes, seven is my hour. I cannot depart
from it, even when travelling; so you see I dare

not. become your guest.   However, I shall see
you daily, and my young cousin here must do
the honours of the neighbourhood to me."

"That I will," said Saxon, heartily.

Mr. Trefalden then shook hands with the
pastor, and, Saxon having declared his intention
of seeing him down the mountain, they went
away together.

CHAPTER VI.

THE VALUE OF A NAPOLEON.

As the two cousins passed across the grass-grown court-yard, and under the gateway with the stork's nest overhead, Mr. Trefalden pointed up to the broken scutcheon.

"Is that a record of some mediæval fray?" asked he.

"Oh dear no!" replied the young man, laughingly. "My great-grandfather smashed that heraldry when he bought the place."

"Then he was a zealous Republican?"

"Not he. Quite the contrary, I believe. No —he defaced the shield because the château was his, and the arms were not."

"I see. He did not choose to live in a house with another man's name upon his door. That was sensible; but he might have substituted his own."

Saxon's lip curled saucily.

"Bah!" said he, "what do we want with arms? We are only farmers. We have no right to them."

"Neither has anyone else, I should fancy, in a republic like this," observed Mr. Trefalden.

"Oh, yes—some have. The Rotzbergs, who lived here before us, the Plantas, the Ortensteins, are all noble. They were counts and knights hundreds of years ago, when the feudal system prevailed."

"Nobles who subscribe to a democratic rule forego their nobility, my young cousin," said Mr. Trefalden.

"I have heard that before," replied Saxon; "but I don't agree with it."

This young man had a sturdy way of expressing his opinions that somewhat amused and somewhat dismayed Mr. Trefalden. He had also a frightful facility of foot that rendered him a difficult companion among such paths as led down from the Château Rotzberg to the valley below.

"My good fellow," said the lawyer, coming to a sudden stop, "do you want me to break my neck?   I'm not a chamois!"

Saxon, who had been springing from ledge to ledge of the slippery descent with the light and fearless step of a mountaineer to the manner born, turned back at once, and put out his hand.

"I beg your pardon," he said, apologetically. "I had forgotten.   I suppose you have never been among mountains before?"

"Oh yes, I have—and I can keep my feet here quite well, thank you, if you do not ask me to come down in a coranto.   I have been up Snowdon, and Cader Idris, and plenty of smaller heights—to say nothing of Holborn Hill."

Saxon laughed merrily.

"Why, what do *you* know of Holborn Hill?" said Mr. Trefalden, surprised to find that small jest appreciated.

"It is a hill rising westward, on the right bank of the Fleet river."

"But you have never visited London?"

"I have never been farther than Zurich in my

life; but I have read Stowe carefully, with a map."

Mr. Trefalden could not forbear a smile.

"You must not suppose that you therefore know anything about modern London," said he. "Stowe would not recognise his own descriptions now. The world has gone round once or twice since his time."

"So I suppose."

"I should like to take you back with me, Saxon. You'd find me a better guide than the mediæval surveyor."

"To London?"

"Ay, to London."

Saxon shook his head.

"You do not mean to tell me that you have no curiosity to visit the most wonderful city in the world?"

"Not at all; but there are others which I had rather see first."

"And which are they?"

"Rome, Athens, and Jerusalem."

"Then I have no hesitation in prophesying that you would be greatly disappointed in all three. One is always disappointed in places that depend for their interest on remote association."

Saxon made no reply, and for a few moments they were both silent. When they presently left the last belt of pines behind them and emerged upon the level road, Mr. Trefalden paused and said :—

"I ought not to let you go any farther. My way lies straight before me now, and I cannot miss it."

"I will go with you as far as the bridge," replied Saxon.

"But it is growing quite dusk, and you have those mountain paths to climb."

"I could climb them blindfold. Besides, we have arranged nothing for to-morrow. Would you like to walk over the Galanda to Pfeffers?"

"How far is it?" asked Mr. Trefalden, with a glance of misgiving towards the mountain in question, which looked loftier than ever in the gloaming.

"About twenty-three or four miles."

"Each way?"

"Of course."

"I am much obliged to you," said the lawyer, "but, as I said before, I am not a chamois. No, Saxon; you must come over to the 'Adler' to-morrow morning to breakfast with me, and after breakfast, if you like, we will walk to Chur. I hear it is a curious old place, and I should like to see it."

"As you please, cousin. At what hour?"

"I fear if I say half-past eight you will think it terribly late."

"Not at all, since you do not dine till seven at night."

"Then I may expect you?"

"Without fail."

They were now within sight of the covered bridge and the twinkling lights in the village beyond. Mr. Trefalden paused for the second time.

"I must insist upon saying good-by now," said he. "And, by the way, before we part, will you be kind enough to explain to me the real value of these coins?"

He took out a handful of loose money, and Saxon examined the pieces by the waning light.

"My charretier to-day would not take French francs," continued Mr. Trefalden, "but asked for Müntz money. When I offered him these Swiss francs he was satisfied. What is the difference in value between a French and a Swiss franc? What is Müntz money? How many of these pieces should I get for a Napoleon, or an English sovereign?"

Saxon shook his head.'

"I don't know," said he. "I have not the least idea."

Mr. Trefalden thought he had been misunderstood.

"I beg your pardon," said he. "Perhaps I have not explained myself clearly. This Müntz money . . ."

"Müntz money is Swiss money," interrupted Saxon. "That is to say, the new uniform coinage voted by the Diet in 1850."

"Well, what is this Swiss franc worth?"

"A hundred rappen."

"Then a rapp is equivalent to a French centime?"

Saxon looked puzzled.

"The rappen are issued instead of the old batzen," said he.

Mr. Trefalden smiled.

"We don't quite understand each other yet," he said, taking a Napoleon from the number. "What I want to know is simply how many Swiss francs I ought to receive for this?"

Saxon took the Napoleon between his finger and thumb, and examined it on both sides with some curiosity.

"I don't think it is worth anything at all here," he replied, as he gave it back. "What is it?"

"What is it! Why, a Napoleon! Do you mean to say that you never saw one before?"

"I don't think I ever did."

"But I know they are current here, for I changed one at Chur."

Saxon looked as if he could not comprehend his cousin's evident surprise.

"You may be right," said he. "I cannot tell; but I will ask my father when I go home. I daresay he can explain it to you."

Mr. Trefalden's amazement was so great that he took no pains to conceal it.

"But, my dear fellow," he said, "you cannot be unacquainted with the standard value of money—with the relative value of gold and silver?"

"I assure you I know nothing at all about it."

"But—but it is incomprehensible."

"Why so? It is a subject which has never come under my observation, and in which I take no interest."

"Yet in the ordinary transactions of life—of farming life, for instance, such as your own—in the common buying and selling of every day . . ."

"I have nothing to do with that. My father manages all matters connected with the land."

"Well, then, if it were only as a guide to the expenditure of your own money, some such knowledge is necessary and valuable."

"But I have no money," replied Saxon, with the simplicity of a savage.

"No money? None whatever?"

"None."

"Do you never have any?"

"Never."

"Have you never had any?"

"Never in my life."

Mr. Trefalden drew a long breath, and said no more.

"That seems to surprise you very much," said Saxon, laughingly.

"Well—it does."

"But it need not. What do I want with money? Of what use would it be to me? What should I do with it? What *is* money? Nothing. Nothing but a sign, the interpretation of which is food, clothing, firing, and other comforts and necessaries of life. I have all these, and, having them, need no money. It is sufficiently plain."

"Ah, yes, it is plain—quite plain," rejoined the lawyer, abstractedly. "I see it all now. You are perfectly right, Saxon. You would not know what to do with it, if you had it. Good night."

"Good night."

"Don't forget half-past eight to-morrow."

"No, no. Good night."

And so they shook hands and parted.

Hastening back to his hotel, Mr. Trefalden

then wrote a few letters before post-time, and
sat down to his solitary table at seven o'clock
precisely. It was a very *recherché* little dinner,
and Mr. Trefalden was unusually well disposed
to enjoy it. Never, surely, was trout more fresh;
never was Mayonnaise better flavoured; never
had Lafitte a more delicate aroma. Mr. Trefalden dined deliberately, praised the cook with
the grace of a connoisseur, and lingered luxuri-
ously over his dessert. His meditations were
pleasant, and the claret was excellent.

"A simple old pastor with a mania for archæology," muttered he, as he sipped his curaçoa
and watched the smoke of his cigar: "a simple
old pastor with a mania for archæology, and a
young barbarian, who reads Theocritus and never
saw a Napoleon! What a delicious combination
of circumstances! What a glorious field for
enterprise! Verily, the days of El Dorado have
come back again!"

CHAPTER VII.

THE pastor had spoken from his heart of hearts
when he told Mr. Trefalden with what solicitude
he had educated his brother's orphan; but he
did not tell him all, or even half, of the zeal,
humility, and devotion with which he had fulfilled
that heavy duty. Knowing the full extent of
his responsibility, he had accepted it from the
very hour of the boy's birth. He had lain awake,
night after night, while little Saxon was yet
in his cradle, pondering and praying, and ask-
ing himself how he should fortify this young
soul against the temptations of the world. He
had written out full a dozen elaborate schemes
of education for him, before the child could
babble an articulate word. He spent his leisure
in studying the lives of great and virtuous men,

that he might thence gather something of their
tutelage; and, to this end, toiled patiently once
again through all Plutarch's crabbed Greek, and
Fuller's still more crabbed English. He com-
piled formidable lists of all kinds of instructive
books for his pupil's future reading, long before
his young ears had ever heard of the penances
ending in "ology." He filled reams of sermon
paper with unobjectionable extracts from the
classic poets, and made easy abstracts of Euclid
and Aristotle for his sole use and benefit. In
short, he laid himself down before the wheels of
this baby Juggernaut in a spirit of the uttermost
self-devotion and love, giving up to him every
moment upon which his pastoral duties held no
claim, and sacrificing even the Etruscans for his
dear sake.

The boy's education may almost be said to
have dated from the day on which he first began
to laugh, and put out his little arms at the sight
of those he loved. Uncle Martin, in spite of
some maternal opposition, took care of that.
He asserted his position at once; and quietly,
but firmly maintained it. He it was who taught

the child his first utterances—who guided his
first feeble steps upon the soft sward out of doors
—who trained his tongue to stammer its first
prayer. He taught him that God had made the
sun, and the stars, and the green trees. He led
him to see use and beauty in all created things
—even in the most unlovely. He brought him
up to fear the darkness no more than the light;
to admire all that was beautiful; to reverence all
that was noble; to love everything that had
life. He would not even let him have a toy that
was not in some way suggestive of gracefulness or
service.

When little Saxon was but two years old, his
mother died; and the good pastor pursued his
labour henceforth without even a semblance of
opposition. Saxon the elder believed in his
brother as of old, and deferred to him in everything. Martin did not, perhaps, believe quite so
implicitly in himself; but, as he told his cousin,
he prayed for light, and only strove to know his
duty, that he might perform it.

As time went on, that duty became daily of
more extensive operation. The boy grew por-

tentously both in ideas and inches. He developed
an alarming appetite for books, as well as bread
and butter. His curiosity became insatiable, and
his industry indefatigable. In short, he perplexed
his tutor sorely, and unconsciously raised up a
host of difficulties which had been left quite un-
provided for in the good pastor's theories.

For Martin Trefalden had theories — very
strange, unworldly, eccentric theories, indeed—
which looked wonderfully well upon paper, and
had been proved by him to his brother over and
over again, as they sat smoking together by their
fireside o' nights; but which had various disagreeable ways of tripping him up and leaving
him in the lurch, now that they came to be put
into practice.

Chief and foremost among these was his grand
theory about the Trefalden legacy.

Having persuaded his brother to marry, and
having, as it were, compelled Saxon the younger
to enter on this stage of mortal life, it obviously
behoved him above all other things to arm that
little Christian against the peculiar dangers and
temptations to which his singular destiny ex-

posed him. He must be trained in habits of innocence, frugality, charity, and self-denial. He must be taught to prize only the simplest pleasures. He must be doubly and trebly fortified against pride, avarice, prodigality, self-indulgence, and every other sin of which wealth is fruitful. Above all, argued the pastor, he must not love money. Nay more, he must be wholly indifferent to it. He must regard it as a mere sign—an expedient—a medium of exchange—a thing valueless in itself, and desirable only because it is convenient. His childish hand must never be sullied by it. His innocent thoughts must never entertain it. He shall be as pure from the taint of gold as the first dwellers in Paradise.

"But when he grows up, brother Martin," suggested the father one evening, while they sat talking it over, as usual, in the chimney corner : "when he grows up, you know, and the money really falls due—what then ? "

" What do you mean, Sax ? "

" He won't know what to do with it."

" But *you* will," replied the pastor, sharply ;

"and, after all, 'tis you are the heir—not he.
You never seem to remember that, brother Sax."

The farmer made no reply.

"And by that time, too," continued Martin,
" the boy will be old enough to understand the
right uses of wealth."

"You'll teach him those, brother Martin," said
the farmer.

"You and I together."

Saxon the elder smoked on in silence for a
moment or two; then, laying his hand gently on
the pastor's sleeve, "Brother Martin," he said,
"thou'rt younger than I, as I have reminded thee
once or twice before. I don't believe that I have
a very long life before me. I don't feel as if I
should ever inherit that fortune, or see my boy
with a beard upon his chin."

He was right. He died, as we know, twelve
years before the century expired, and Martin
Trefalden continued to bring up his nephew in
his own way. He could ride his hobby now at
any pace he pleased, without even the interruption
of a meek question by the way; so he ambled on
year after year with his eyes shut, and refused to

recognise the fact that Saxon was no longer a
boy.   He made himself wilfully blind both to his
moustache and his inches.   He would not believe
that the time was already come for discussing the
forbidden subject.   He could not endure to tell
his young Spartan that he must one day be rich;
and so, as it were, be the first to raise his hand
against that fabric of unworldliness which it had
been the labour of his life to erect.

Of late, however, he had "had misgivings."
He had begun to wonder whether perfect ignorance of life was really the best preparation for a
career of usefulness, and whether the college at
Geneva might not have proved a better school
for his nephew than the solitude of Domleschg.

Thus matters stood when William Trefalden,
Esquire, of Chancery Lane, London, made his
appearance at the Château Rotzberg; and thus it
happened that his cousin Saxon, the heir to four
millions and a half of funded property, had no
notion of the value of a Napoleon.

CHAPTER VIII.

PUNCTUAL as the minute hand of the quaint little Swiss timepiece on the mantelshelf, was Saxon to his appointment. The first metallic chime of the half-hour was just striking as he reached the inn door, and the rapid smiting of his iron heel on the paved corridor leading to the salon drowned the vibrations of the second. He found the breakfast-table laid beside a window looking upon the garden and the mountains, and his cousin turning over the leaves of a large book at the farther end of the room.

"It is pleasant to find one's self so good a judge of character," said Mr. Trefalden, advancing with outstretched hand. "I felt sure you would be true to time, Saxon—*so* sure, that I had sent

the eggs away to be poached—and here they are !
Come, sit down. I hope you're hungry."

" Indeed I am," replied Saxon, making a
vigorous onslaught upon the loaf.

" You seem to have brought the mountain air
in with you," said Mr. Trefalden, with a half-
envious glance at his fresh young cheek and
breezy curls. " It is a glorious morning for
walking."

" That it is; and I have been up to some of
the high pastures in search of one of our goats.
It was so clear at six o'clock that I saw the
Glärnisch quite plainly."

" What is the Glärnisch—a mountain ? "

" Yes—a splendid mountain ; the highest in the
Canton Glarus."

" What wine do you prefer, Saxon ? "

" Oh, either, thank you. I like the one as well
as the other."

Mr. Trefalden raised his eyes from the *carte
des vins*.

" What 'one' and what 'other' do you mean ?"
asked he.

" The red and the white."

"You mean vin ordinaire?"

"Certainly. Why not?"

Mr. Trefalden shrugged his shoulders.

"I don't drink vinegar myself," said he, "and I should not choose to place it before you. We will try a bottle of our host's Château Margaux. I suppose you like that?"

"I don't know," replied Saxon. "I never tasted it."

"Have you ever tasted champagne?"

"Never."

"Would you like to do so?"

"Indeed I don't care. I like one thing just as well as another. These cutlets are capital."

Mr. Trefalden looked at his cousin with an expression of mingled wonder and compassion.

"My dear boy," said he, "what have you done, that you should *only* like one thing as well as another?"

Saxon looked puzzled.

"It is a shocking defect, either of constitution or education," continued Mr. Trefalden, gravely. "You must try to get over it. Don't laugh. I am perfectly serious. Here, taste this pâté, and tell me if you like it *only* as well as the cutlets."

Saxon tasted it, and made a wry face.

"What is it made of?" said he. "What are those nasty black things in it?"

"It is a pâté de foie gras," replied Mr. Trefalden, pathetically, "and those nasty black things are truffles—the greatest delicacies imaginable."

Saxon laughed heartily, poured some claret into a tumbler, and put out his hand for the water-bottle.

"You are not going to mix that Château Margaux!" cried Mr. Trefalden.

"Why not?"

"Because it is sacrilege to spoil the flavour."

"But I am thirsty."

"So much the better. Your palate is all the more susceptible. Try the first glass pure, at all events."

Saxon submitted, and emptied his glass at a draught.

"That *is* delicious," said he.

"You really think so?"

"Unquestionably."

"You prefer it to the vin ordinaire?"

"I do, indeed."

Mr. Trefalden drew a deep breath of satisfaction.

"*Allons!*" said he. "Then there is some little
hope for you, Saxon, after all."

"But . . . "

"But what?"

Saxon hesitated.

"But I am not sure," said he, "that I prefer
it to the vin d'Asti."

Mr. Trefalden leaned back in his chair and
groaned aloud.

"I'm sure I'm very sorry," laughed Saxon,
with a comic look, half shy, half penitent. "But
—but it isn't my fault, is it?"

Before Mr. Trefalden could reply to this appeal,
there was a rustling of silk, and a sound of voices
in the corridor, and a lady and gentleman entered
the salon, conversing earnestly. Seeing others in
the room, they checked themselves. In the same
instant Mr. Trefalden, who sat partly turned
towards the door, rose and exclaimed:—

"Mademoiselle Colonna!"

The lady put out her hand.

"You here, Mr. Trefalden?" said she. "*Padre mio,* you remember Mr. Trefalden?"

The gentleman, who held his hat in one hand and a bundle of letters and papers in the other, bowed somewhat distantly, and said he believed he had had the pleasure of meeting Mr. Trefalden before.

"Yes, at Castletowers," replied the lawyer.

The gentleman's dark face lighted up instantly, and, laying his hat aside, he also advanced to shake hands.

"Forgive me," he said, "I did not remember that you were a friend of Lord Castletowers. Have you seen him lately? I hope you are well. This is a charming spot. Have you been here long? We have only this moment arrived."

He asked questions without waiting for replies, and spoke hurriedly and abstractedly, as if his thoughts were busy elsewhere all the time. Both his accent and his daughter's were slightly foreign, but his was more foreign than hers.

"I only came yesterday," replied Mr. Trefalden, "and I propose to stay here for a week or

two.   May one venture to hope that you are
about to do the same?"

The young lady shook her head. Her father
had already moved away to the opposite side of
the room, and was examining his letters.

"We are only waiting to breakfast while our
vetturino feeds his horses," said she; "and we
hope to reach Chur in time for the midday train."

"A short sojourn," said Mr. Trefalden.

"Yes; I am sorry for it. We have travelled
by this road very often, and always in haste. The
place, I am sure, would repay investigation. It
is very beautiful."

"You come from Italy, I suppose?"

"Yes, from Milan."

"And are, of course, as devoted as ever to the
good cause?"

Her eyes seemed to flash and dilate as she
lifted them suddenly upon her interrogator.

"You know, Mr. Trefalden," said she, "that
we live for no other. But why do *you* call it the
'good' cause? You have never joined us—you
have never helped us. I had no idea that you
deemed it a good cause."

"Then you did me injustice," replied the lawyer, with an unembarrassed smile. "The liberty and unity of a great people must be a good cause. I should blush for my opinions if I did not think so."

"Then why not give us the support of your name?"

"Because, my dear madam, it would bring no support with it. I am an obscure man. I have neither wealth nor influence."

"Even if that were so, it would be of little importance," said Mademoiselle Colonna, eagerly. "Every volunteer is precious—even the humblest and weakest. But you are neither, Mr. Trefalden. You are far from being an obscure man. You are a very brilliant man—nay, I mean no compliment. I only repeat what I have often heard. I know that you have talent, and I am sure you are not without influence. You would be a most welcome accession to our staff."

"Indeed, Mademoiselle Colonna, you over-estimate me in every way."

"I do not think so."

"I ought also to tell you that I am a very

busy man. My whole life is absorbed by my professional duties."

"It is always possible to find time for good deeds," replied the lady.

"I fear, not always."

"*Enfin*, we are not exacting. To those friends who can give us but their names and their sympathies, we are grateful. You will be one of those, I am sure."

"It is better to give nothing, than to give that which is worthless," said Mr. Trefalden.

Mademoiselle Colonna met this reply with a slight curl of the lip, and another flash of her magnificent eyes.

"Those who are not for Italy, are against her, Mr. Trefalden," she said coldly, and turned away.

The lawyer recovered his position with perfect tact.

"I cannot allow Mademoiselle Colonna to mistake me a second time," he said. "If she does me the honour to value my poor name at more than its worth, I can but place it at her disposal."

"Are you sincere?" she said, quickly.

" Undoubtedly."

" You permit us the use of your name ? "

Mr. Trefalden smiled, and bent his head.

" Thanks in the name of the cause."

" But, signora . . ."

" But what ? "

" You will forgive me if I desire to know in what manner you propose to make my name serviceable ? "

" I shall enter it on our general committee list."

" Is that all ? "

" All—neither more nor less."

Mr. Trefalden's face showed neither satisfaction nor dissatisfaction. It was perfectly placid and indifferent, like his smile. Mademoiselle Colonna looked at him as if she would read him through ; but she could do nothing of the kind.

" If you repent of the permission you have granted," she began, " or object to the publicity of . . ."

" No, no," interposed the lawyer, with a little deprecatory raising of the hand, " not at all. It gives me much pleasure."

" If, then, on the contrary, you choose at any time to favour us with more active aid," continued she, " you need only write to my father, or Lord Castletowers, or, indeed, to any of the honorary secretaries, and your co-operation will meet with grateful and immediate acceptance. Till then, no demand will be made upon your time or patience."

Mr. Trefalden bowed.

" Have you many such drones in your hive, signora ? " asked he.

" Hundreds."

" But they only can be incumbrances."

" Quite the contrary. They are of considerable value. Their names give weight to our cause in the eyes of the world ; and the printed lists which contain them find their way into every court and cabinet in Europe. For instance, I have here a paper——"

She paused, glanced towards Saxon, and dropping her voice almost to a whisper, said :—

" Your guide, I suppose ? Does he understand English ? "

" Perfectly," replied Mr. Trefalden, answering

the second question, and taking no notice of the
first. " As well as you, or myself."

" *Dio!* Have I said too much? Is he safe?"

" I would answer for him with my head, if
even he had understood the purport of our conversation—which he has not done."

" How can you be sure of that? "

" Because he is a wild mountaineer, and knows
no more of politics than you, Signora Colonna,
know of the common law of England."

The young lady took a folded paper from her
pocket, and placed it in Mr. Trefalden's hand.

" Read that," she said. " It is from Rome.
You are aware, of course, that Sardinia——"

Her voice fell again to a whisper. She drew
the lawyer away to her father's table, spread the
document before him, and proceeded to comment
upon its contents. This she did with great
earnestness and animation, but in a tone of voice
audible only to her listener. Mr. Trefalden was
all attention. Signor Colonna, his thin hands
twisted in his hair, and his elbows resting on the
table, remained absorbed in his papers. Saxon,
who had not presumed to lift his eyes from his

plate while the lady stood near him, ventured to
glance now and then towards the group at the
farther end of the room. Having looked once,
he looked again, and could not forbear looking. It was not at all strange that he should
do so. On the contrary, it would have been
strange if he had done otherwise; for Saxon
Trefalden was gifted with a profound, almost a
religious, sense of beauty, and he had never in
his life seen anything so beautiful as Olimpia
Colonna.

CHAPTER IX.

SAXON TREFALDEN did not fall in love at first sight, as Palamon fell in love with Emelie, walking in the garden "full of braunches grene." His heart beat none the faster, his cheek grew none the brighter, or the paler, for that stolen contemplation. Nothing of the kind. He only admired her—admired her, and wondered at her, and delighted to look upon her; just as he would have admired, and wondered at, and looked upon a gorgeous sunrise among his own native Alps, or a splendid meteor in a summer sky. He did not attempt to analyse her features. He could not have described her to save his life. He had no idea whether her wondrous eyes were brown or black; or whether it was to them, or to the perfect mouth beneath, that her smile owed the

magic of its sweetness. He had not the faintest
suspicion that her hair was of the same hue and
texture as the world-famed locks of Lucrezia
Borgia; he only saw that it was tossed back from
her brow like a cloud of burnt gold, crisp and
wavy, and gathered into a coronet that a queen
might have envied. He knew not how scornfully
her lip could curl, and her delicate nostrils
quiver; but he could not help seeing how there
was something haughty in the very undulations
of her tall and slender form, and something imperial in the character of her beauty. In short,
Saxon was no connoisseur of female loveliness.
The women of the Grisons are among the home-
liest of their race, and till now he had seen no
others. A really graceful, handsome, highly-bred
woman was a phenomenon in his eyes; and he
looked upon her with much the same kind of
delightful awe that one experiences on first be-
holding the sea, or the southern stars. Indeed,
had Mademoiselle Colonna been only a fine portrait by Titian, or a marble divinity by Phidias,
he could hardly have admired her with a more
dispassionate and simple wonder.

Presently Mr. Trefalden came back to his breakfast, leaving Signor Colonna and his daughter to theirs. He resumed his seat in silence. He looked grave. He pushed his plate aside with the air of one whose thoughts are too busy for hunger. Then he looked at Saxon; but Saxon's eyes were wandering to the farther end of the salon, and he knew nothing of the close and serious scrutiny to which he was being subjected. The young man would, perhaps, have been somewhat startled had he surprised that expression upon his cousin's face; and even more puzzled than startled by the strange, flitting, cynical smile into which it gradually faded.

"Come, Saxon," said Mr. Trefalden, "we must finish this bottle of Château Margaux before we go."

Saxon shook his head.

"You have had only one glass," remonstrated his cousin.

"Thank you, I do not wish for more."

"Then you don't really like it, after all?"

"Yes, I do; but I am no longer thirsty. See —I have almost emptied the water-bottle."

Mr. Trefalden shrugged his shoulders.

"We are told," said he, "that primæval man passed through three preliminary stages before he reached the era of civilisation—namely, the stone period, the iron period, and the bronze. You, my dear Saxon, are still in the stone period; and Heaven only knows how long you might have stayed there, if I had not come to your aid! It is my mission to civilise you."

Saxon laughed aloud. It was his way to laugh on the smallest provocation, like a joyous child; which, in Mr. Trefalden's eyes, was another proof of barbarianism.

"Civilise me, as much as you please, cousin William," he said: "but don't ask me to drink without thirst, or eat without hunger."

Mr. Trefalden glanced uneasily towards the other table, where the father and daughter were breakfasting side by side, and conversing softly in Italian. Perhaps he did not wish them to hear Saxon call him "cousin." At all events, he rose abruptly, and said :—

"Come—shall we smoke a cigar in the garden before starting?"

But just as they were leaving the room, Mademoiselle Colonna rose and followed them.

"Mr. Trefalden," she said eagerly, "Mr. Trefalden—we found letters awaiting us at this place, one of which demands an immediate answer. This answer must be conveyed to a certain spot, by a trusty messenger. It may not, for various reasons, be sent through the post. Can you help me? Do you know of any person whom it would be safe to employ?"

"Indeed I do not," replied the lawyer. "I am as great a stranger in Reichenau as yourself. Perhaps, however, the landlord can tell you . . ."

"No, no," interrupted she. "It will not be prudent to consult him."

"Then I fear I am powerless."

"It—it is not very far," hesitated the lady. "He would only have to go about a mile beyond Thusis, on the Splugen road."

"If I were not a man of law, Mademoiselle Colonna," said Mr. Trefalden, with his blandest smile, "I would myself volunteer to be your envoy; but . . ."

"But you have given us your name, Mr. Tre-falden, and can do no more. I understand that. I understood it from the first. I am only sorry to have troubled you."

"And I am sorry that you have not troubled me. I regret that I cannot be of more ser-vice."

Wherewith Mr. Trefalden bowed to Mademoi-selle Colonna, made a sign to his cousin to follow him, and left the room. But Saxon lingered, blushing and irresolute, and turned to the lady instead.

"I can take the letter," he said, shyly.

Mademoiselle Colonna paused, looked straight into his eyes, and said——

"It is an important letter. Can I trust you?"

"Yes."

"Can I rely upon you to give it into no other hands than those of the person whom I shall describe to you?"

"Yes."

"If anyone else should try to take it from you, what would you do?"

"If a man tried to take it from me by force,"

replied Saxon, laughingly, "I should knock him down."

"But if he were stronger than you; or if there were several?"

He stopped to consider.

"I—I think I should take it out, as if I were going to give it up," said he, "and I would swallow it."

"Good."

Mademoiselle Colonna paused again, and again looked at him steadfastly.

"Did you hear all that I said about this letter just now to Mr. Trefalden?" she said.

"Every word of it."

"You know that you must not repeat it?"

"I suppose so."

"And you know that to convey this letter may be—though it is very unlikely—a service of some little danger?"

"I did not know that; but I knew it was a service of responsibility."

"Well, then, are you equally willing to go?"

"Of course. Why not?"

Mademoiselle Colonna smiled, but somewhat doubtfully.

"I do not doubt your courage," she said; "but how am I to know that you will not betray my confidence?"

Saxon coloured up to the roots of his hair, and drew back a step.

"You must not give me the letter," said he, "if you are afraid to trust me. I can only promise to deliver it, and be silent."

Signor Colonna rose suddenly, and joined them. He had his purse in his hand.

"Will you swear this, young man?" he asked. "Will you swear this?"

"No," said Saxon, proudly, "I will not swear it. It is forbidden to take God's name for trifles. I will give you my word of honour, but I will not take an oath."

"Humph! what reward do you expect?"

"Reward? What do you mean?"

"Will twenty francs satisfy you?"

Saxon drew back another step. He looked from Signor Colonna to his daughter, and from the lady's face to the gentleman's.

"Money!" he faltered. "You offer me money?"

"Is it not enough?"

Barbarian as he was, Saxon was quite sufficiently civilised to writhe under the sting of this affront. The tears started to his honest eyes. It was the first humiliation he had known in his life, and he felt it bitterly.

"I did not offer to carry your letter for hire," said he, in a hurried, quivering voice. "I would have gone twice the distance to—to please and serve the lady. Good morning."

And, turning abruptly on his heel, the young man strode out of the room.

"Oh, stay, monsieur, one moment—one moment only!" cried Mademoiselle Colonna.

But he was already gone.

"What is this? Who is he? What does it all mean?" asked Signor Colonna, impatiently.

"It means that we have committed a grievous error," replied his daughter. "He is a gentleman—a gentleman, and I took him for a common guide! But see, there he goes, through the garden gate—go to him; pray go to him, and apologise in my name and your own."

"But, my child," said the Italian, nervously, "how can you be sure . . . ?"

"I am sure. I see it all now—I ought to have seen it from the first. But look yonder, and convince yourself! Mr. Trefalden has taken his arm—they go down through the trees! Pray go—go at once, or you will be too late!"

Signor Colonna snatched up his hat and went at once; but he was too late for all that. The garden was a very perplexing place. It belonged, not to the hotel, but to the Château Planta close by, and was entered by a large iron gate, some few yards down the road. It was laid out on a little picturesque peninsula just at the junction of the Hinter and Vorder Rhines, and was traversed by all kinds of winding walks, some of which led down to the water side, some up to retired nooks, or hidden summer-houses, or open lawns fragrant with violets, and musical with ever-playing fountains. Up and down, in and out of these paths, Signor Colonna wandered for nearly half-an-hour without meeting a living soul, or hearing any sound but the rushing of the rivers and the echoes of his own steps on the gravel. Saxon and his cousin had disappeared as utterly as if the green sward had opened and swallowed them, or the grey Rhine had swept them away in its eddying current.

CHAPTER X.

PASTOR MARTIN never closed his eyes in sleep that night after William Trefalden paid his first visit at the Château Rotzberg. His anxieties had been increasing and multiplying of late, and this event brought them *en masse* to the surface. He scarcely knew whether to feel relieved or embarrassed by the arrival of his London kinsman. Harassed as his mind had been for some time past, he yet dreaded to lay the source of his troubles before an arbiter who might tell him that he had acted unwisely. Yet here was the arbiter, dropped, as it were, from the clouds; and, be his verdict what it might, the story of Saxon's education could not be withheld from him. The good priest shrunk from this confession. It was true that he had done all for the

best. It was also true that he would have given
his own life to make that boy a good and happy
man. And yet—and yet there remained the
fatal possibility which had so haunted him during
these last few months. His own judgment might
all this time have been at fault; and the fair
edifice which he had been building up with such
love and devotion for the last twenty years or
more, might, after all, have its foundations in the
sand. This was a terrible thought—a thought so
hard to bear that the pastor made up his mind
to go down to Reichenau early in the morning,
and talk the whole matter over with William
Trefalden, before he and Saxon should have
started for Chur. When the morning came,
however, a goat was missing from the flock.
This mischance threw all the farm-work out of
its daily course, so that the pastor started a good
half-hour too late, quite expecting to find them
both gone by the time he reached the Adler.

In the meanwhile, Saxon had overtaken his
cousin in the garden of the Château Planta.

"Well," said Mr. Trefalden, "I began to
think you were never coming. Take a cigar?"

L 2

Saxon shook his head.

" I don't smoke, thank you," said he hurriedly.
" This way."

Mr. Trefalden noted the flush upon his cheek,
and the agitation of his manner, and followed in
silence.

The young man plunged down a labyrinth of
narrow side walks, till they came to one that
sloped to the water-side. At the bottom of this
slope, only a wire fence and a slip of gravelly
bank lay between them and the river. A covered
bridge spanned the stream a few yards higher up,
and beyond the bridge lay the meadows and the
mountains. Saxon, without deigning to touch
the wire with his hand, sprang lightly over.
Mr. Trefalden, less lightly, and more leisurely,
followed his example. In a few minutes more,
they had both passed through the gloom of the
covered bridge, and emerged into the sunshine
beyond. Saxon at once struck across the road,
and took the field path opposite.

" Is this the way to Chur?" asked Mr. Trefalden, somewhat abruptly.

Saxon started, and stopped.

"No, indeed," he replied. "I—I had forgotten. We must turn back."

"Not till I have finished my cigar. See—here is an old pine-trunk, that looks as if it had been felled on purpose. Let us sit and chat quietly for half-an-hour."

"With all my heart," said Saxon. So they sat down side by side, far enough out of sight or hearing of the garden in which Signor Colonna was searching for them on the opposite side of the river.

"By the way, Saxon, what kept you so long, just now?" said Mr. Trefalden. "Were you flirting with the fair Olimpia?"

Saxon's face was scarlet in an instant.

"I—I offered to carry her letter," he replied, confusedly.

"The deuce you did! And she declined?"

"She misunderstood me."

"I am heartily glad of it. I would not have had you mixed up in any of the Colonna intrigues for a trifle. In what way did she misunderstand you?"

Saxon bit his lip, and the colour which

had nearly faded from his face came back again.

"She thought I wanted to be paid for going," he said, reluctantly.

"Offered you money, in short?"

"Yes—that is, her father did so."

"And what did you say?"

"I hardly know. I was greatly vexed—more vexed, perhaps, than I ought to have been. I left them, at all events, and here I am."

"Without the letter, I trust?"

"Without the letter."

There was a brief silence. Mr. Trefalden looked down thoughtfully, and a faint smile flitted over his face. Saxon did not see it. His thoughts were busy elsewhere, and his eyes were also bent upon the ground.

"I am sorry you don't join me," said Mr. Trefalden. "Smoking is a social art, and you should acquire it."

"The art is easy enough," said Saxon. "It is the taste for it which is difficult of acquisition."

"Then you have tried it?"

"Yes."

"And it made you giddy?"

"Not at all; but it gave me no pleasure."

"That was because you did not persevere long enough to experience the delicious dreaminess that ..."

"I have no desire to feel dreamy," interrupted Saxon. "I should detest any sensation that left my mind less active than usual. I had as soon put on fetters."

Mr. Trefalden laughed that low, pleasant laugh of his, and stretched himself at full length on the grass.

"There are fetters, and fetters," said he. "Fetters of gold, and fetters of flowers, as well as fetters of vulgar iron."

"Heaven forbid that I should ever know any of the three," observed Saxon, gravely.

"You have this very day been in danger of the two last," replied Mr. Trefalden.

"Cousin, you are jesting."

"Cousin, I am doing nothing of the kind."

Saxon's blue eyes opened in amazement.

"What *can* you mean?" said he.

"I will tell you. But you must promise to

listen patiently, for my explanation involves some
amount of detail."

Saxon bent his head, and the lawyer, puffing
lazily at his cigar from time to time, continued.

"The Colonna family," said he, "is, as of
course you know already, one of the oldest and
noblest of the princely Roman houses. Giulio
Colonna, whom you saw just now at the Adler, is
a scion of the stock. He has been an enthusiast
all his life. In his youth he married for love;
and, for the last twenty or thirty years, has
devoted himself, heart and soul, to Italian
politics. He has written more pamphlets and
ripened more plots than any man in Europe.
He is at the bottom of every Italian conspiracy.
He is at the head of every secret society that has
Italian unity for its object. He is, in short, a
born agitator; and his daughter is as fanatical
as himself. As you saw them just now, so they
are always. He with his head full of plots, and
his pockets full of pamphlets—she exercising all
her woman's wit and energy to enlist or utilise an
ally."

"I understand now what she meant by the 'good cause,'" observed Saxon, thoughtfully.

"Ay, that's the hackneyed phrase."

Saxon looked up.

"But it *is* a good cause," said he. "It is the liberty of her country."

Mr. Trefalden shrugged his shoulders.

"Yes, yes, of course it is," he replied; "but one gets weary of this pamphleteering and plotting. Fighting is one thing, Saxon, and intriguing, another. Besides, I hate a female politician."

"She is very beautiful," said Saxon.

"She is beautiful, and brilliant, and very fascinating; and she knows how to employ her power, too. Those eyes of Olimpia Colonna's have raised more volunteers for Italy than all her father's pamphlets. Confess now, would you have been so ready to carry that letter this morning, if the lady had worn blue spectacles and a front?"

"I cannot tell, but I fear not," replied the young man, laughingly. "But what has this to do with the fetters?"

"Everything. Granted, now, that the fair signora had known you were my cousin . . . "

"I suppose she took me for your servant," interposed Saxon, somewhat bitterly.

"——and that you had really taken charge of that paper grenade," continued Mr. Trefalden, "can you not guess what the results might have been? Well, I can. She would not have offered you money—not a *sous*—but she would have smiled upon you, and given you her hand at parting; and you would probably have kissed it as if she had been an empress, and worshipped her as if she were a divinity; and your head, my dear Saxon, would have been as irretrievably turned as the heads of the false prophets in Dante's seventh circle."

"No, that it would not," said Saxon, hastily; with his face all on fire again at the supposition. "And besides, the false prophets were in the eighth circle, cousin—the place, you know, called Malebolge."

"True—the eighth. Thank you. Then you would have placed the grenade in whichever pocket lay nearest to the place where your heart used to be; and you would have gone to the world's end as readily as to Thusis; and have been abjectly happy to wear Mademoiselle Colonna's fetters of flowers for the rest of your natural life."

"Nay, but indeed . . ."

"So much for the flowers," interrupted Mr. Trefalden. "Now for the iron. Once embarked in this 'good cause,' there would have been no hope for you in the future. In less than a month, you would have been affiliated to some secret society. Dwelling as you do, on the high road to Italy, you would have been appointed to all kinds of dangerous services; and the result of the whole affair would have been an Austrian dungeon, whence not even Santa Olimpia herself would have power to extricate you."

"A very pleasant picture, and very well painted," said Saxon, with an angry quiver of the lip; "but an error, cousin, from beginning to end. I should have devoted myself neither to the lady nor the cause; so your argument falls to the ground, and the fetters along with it."

Mr. Trefalden had too much tact to pursue

the conversation further, so he changed the
subject.

"Are you fond of music?" he asked.

"Passionately."

"Do you play any instrument?"

"I play a little on our chapel organ, but very
badly."

"By ear, I suppose?"

"Not entirely. My father learned music at
Geneva, in his youth; and all that he knows he
has taught me."

"Which, I suppose," said Mr. Trefalden, "is
just enough to make you wish it were more?"

"Precisely."

"Have you a good organ at the chapel?"

"No, a wretched thing. It is very small, very
old, and sadly out of repair. Two of the stops
are quite useless, and there are but five altogether."

"A wretched thing, indeed! Can't you get a
new one?"

"I fear not. Perhaps when Count Planta
comes back from Italy he may give us one. My
father means to mention it to him, at all events;

but then the count is always either in Naples or
Paris. He may not come to Reichenau for the
next three or four years."

"And in the meanwhile," said Mr. Trefalden,
"the organ may die of old age, and become
altogether dumb."

"Quite true," replied Saxon with a sigh.

Mr. Trefalden glanced at him sharply, and a
silence of some moments ensued.

"Don't you think, Saxon," said he, at length,
"that it must be very pleasant to be rich?"

Saxon looked up from his reverie, and smiled.

"To be rich?" he repeated.

"Ay—as Count Planta, for instance."

"Are you serious, cousin?"

"Quite serious."

"Then I think it cannot be pleasant at all."

"Why not?"

"Because wealth is power, and power is a
frightful temptation."

"Nonsense!" said Mr. Trefalden.

"And a frightful responsibility, too."

"Nonsense again!"

"All history proves it," said Saxon, earnestly.

"Look at Athens and Rome—see how luxury undermined the liberty of the one, and how the desire of aggrandisement . . ."

Mr. Trefalden laid his hand laughingly upon the young man's mouth.

"My dear fellow," said he, "you talk like a class-book, or an Exeter Hall lecturer! Who cares about Rome or Athens now? One would think you were a thousand years old, at the very least."

"But . . ."

"But your arguments are very true, and classical, and didactic—I grant all that. Nevertheless our daily experience proves money to be a remarkably agreeable thing. You, I think, are rather proud of your poverty."

"I am not poor." replied Saxon. "I have all that I need. An emperor can have no more."

"Humph! Are there no poor in Reichenau?"

"None who are very poor. None so poor as the people of Embs."

"Where is Embs?"

"About half-way on the road to Chur. It is a

Roman Catholic parish, and the inhabitants are miserably squalid and idle."

"I remember the place. I passed it on my way here yesterday. It looked like a hotbed of fever."

"And well it might," replied Saxon, sadly. "They had it terribly last autumn."

Mr. Trefalden faced round suddenly, leaning on his elbow, and flung away the end of his cigar.

"And so you think, young man," said he, "that because you have all you need, money would be of no use to you! Pray, did it never occur to you that these fever-stricken wretches wanted food, medicine, and clothing?"

"We—we did what we could, cousin," replied Saxon, in a troubled voice. "God knows it was very little, but ..."

"But if you had been a rich man, you could have done ten times more. Is that not true?"

"Too true."

"Your religion enjoins you to give alms; but how are you to do this without money?"

"One may do good works without money," said Saxon.

"In a very limited degree. Not one-tenth part as many as if you had plenty of it. Did you never look at that side of the question, Saxon? Did you never wish to be rich for the sake of others?"

"I am not sure, but I do not think I ever did. I was so impressed with the belief that money was the root of all evil . . ."

"Pshaw! Things are good or evil according to the use we make of them. A knife is but a knife, whether in the hand of a surgeon or an assassin; yet the result is considerably different. You must divest your mind of these fallacies, Saxon. They are unworthy of you!"

Saxon put his hand to his brow uneasily.

"What you say sounds like the truth," said he; "and yet—and yet it is at variance with the precepts upon which I have relied all my life."

"Very possibly," replied Mr. Trefalden. "Precepts, however, are bad things to depend upon. They are made of india-rubber, and will stretch to cover any proposition. Let us suppose, now, that you were a rich man . . ." ,

" How absurd!" said Saxon, forcing a smile.
" What is the use of it?"

" We will see what might have been the use of
it. In the first place you would have had good
instruction, and have become an accomplished
musician. You would have enriched yonder little
church with a fine organ, and perhaps have re-
built the church into the bargain. You would
have furnished the poor sufferers of Embs with a
staff of doctors and nurses, and have saved, perhaps, some scores of human lives. You would
have been able to surround your uncle with comforts in his old age. You could have gratified
your desire of visiting Rome, Athens, and Jerusalem. You could have lined the old château
from top to bottom with Greek and Latin poets,
and have founded a museum of Etruscan antiquities for your uncle's perpetual delight.
Finally——"

He paused. Saxon looked up.

" Well, cousin," said he; " finally what?"

" Finally, rich men do not wear grey blouses
and leather gaiters. If you had had a coat like
mine on your back this morning, Saxon, Made-

moiselle Colonna would not have taken you for a common peasant, and Signor Colonna would not have offered you money."

Saxon sprang to his feet with an impatient gesture.

"Enough of would be, and might be!" exclaimed he. "Of what use are these speculations? I am not rich, and I never shall be rich; so it is idle to think of it."

"At all events," persisted Mr. Trefalden, "you admit the desirableness of wealth?"

"I—I am not sure. I cannot relinquish an old belief so hastily."

"Not even in favour of the truth?"

"I do not yet know that it is the truth. My mind needs further evidence."

"Of what, my son?" said a gentle voice close behind him.

It was the pastor. There was a field path across those very meadows between Rotzberg and Reichenau, and the pine-trunk where the cousins had stayed to rest lay within a dozen yards of its course.

Saxon uttered a joyous exclamation.

"This is fortunate!" cried he. "You come at the right moment, father, to judge our argument."

"We were talking of riches," said Mr. Trefalden, rising, and grasping the old man's outstretched hand. "My young kinsman here preaches the language of an Arcadian, and declaims against the precious metals like a second Timon. I, on the other hand, have been trying to convince him that gold has a very bright side, indeed, and may be made to perform a good many wise offices. What say you?"

The pastor looked distressed.

"The question is a broad one," said he, "and there is much truth on both sides of it. But we cannot discuss it now. I want to talk to you, Cousin William. I have hastened down from Rotzberg, fearing all the time lest I should miss you. Were you not going to Chur?"

"We were going, and are going, by-and-by," replied Mr. Trefalden.

"Can you spare me half-an-hour before you start?"

"The whole day, if you please."

M 2

"Nay, an hour will be more than enough. Saxon, that which I have to say to our cousin is not for thy ears. Go up, my son, to Tamins, and inquire about that Indian corn-seed that farmer Retzschel promised us last week."

Saxon looked surprised; but prepared to be gone without a word.

"Shall I come back here afterwards?" he asked.

"No. It would be better to await thy cousin at the Adler."

Saxon hesitated.

"Could I not wait at the chapel?" said he.

"Ay, at the chapel, if thou wilt."

So the young man waved a cheery farewell, and started at once upon his uncle's errand. Looking back presently, at the turn of the path, he saw them sitting on the pine-trunk, side by side, already in earnest conversation. He saw Mr. Trefalden shake his head. He fancied there was some kind of trouble in the old man's attitude. What could his uncle have to say to one whom, kinsman though he was, he had never seen till the previous evening? Why this mystery about

their conversation ? It was very strange. Saxon
could not help feeling that he must be himself
concerned, somehow or another, in the matter;
and this surmise added, vaguely, to his uneasiness.

CHAPTER XI.

UP AT THE CHURCH.

THREE hours later, Saxon was sitting alone before the organ in the little chapel on the hill. One hand supported his head, the other rested listlessly upon the keys. A tattered mass of Palestrina's lay open upon the music desk; but Saxon's eyes were turned towards the door, and his thoughts were far away. He had been playing half an hour or an hour ago, and had fallen since then into a long and anxious train of thought. He had even forgotten the little fair-haired urchin who acted for him as blower, and who had fallen fast asleep in the sunshine that streamed through the window at the back of the organ.

It was a plain, white-washed, brown-raftered little church, with a row of deal benches on each

side of the aisle, and a pulpit to match. On a
long board suspended from the roof just above
the altar was painted, in gaudy characters of gold
and scarlet, a German couplet, signifying " Where
God is, there is liberty." The organ was of old
dark oak, with ebony keys; and on the top stood
a battered angel with a broken trumpet. It was
a place of primitive simplicity, and no kind of
architectural beauty. The beauty lay all without,
among the Alps and pine forests that showed here
and there through open doors and windows.

It was more than an hour past mid-day when
Saxon Trefalden sat thus before the organ, and
his cousin had not yet come to claim his company.
His thoughts were busy, and his soul was dis-
quieted within him. The uneasiness that he had
felt on leaving those two to their solitary conference had now increased tenfold. Why was he
excluded from it? And why should his uncle,
who had never, as he believed, hidden a thought
from him before, keep a secret from him now?

Then, what of this unknown kinsman, William
Trefalden of London? Did Saxon really like
him? The question was a difficult one. He

scarcely knew how to answer it, even to himself.
He thought he liked his cousin. Nay, he felt
sure—almost sure—that he liked him. Not,
perhaps, quite so well to-day as yesterday. Was
it that an indefinite sense of mistrust mingled
with the liking? No, that was impossible. His
generous nature revolted at the thought. Was
it that William Trefalden's opinions were so new
to him, and went so far to unsettle his own pre-
conceived notions of good and evil? Or was it that
he was himself somewhat out of humour with the
world this morning—somewhat less contented
than of old? The organ, to be sure, had sounded
more wheezy and thin than ever to-day, and his
own playing had seemed clumsier than usual.
Besides, that matter of the twenty francs was
hard to forget. Well, well, he certainly liked his
cousin; and as for poverty, why he must put up
with it, and make the best of it, as his father and
uncle had done before him! Then, with regard
to Olimpia Colonna——Pshaw! were she fair as
Helen, and patriotic as Camilla, it would make
no difference to him. Saxon flattered himself
that he was invulnerable.

At this point of his meditations, a shadow fell upon the threshold, and was followed by the substance of William Trefalden.

"I am ashamed, Saxon," said he, "to have kept you waiting for me so long. Your uncle is gone home, and I suppose it is too late to think of Chur to-day. Is this the organ?"

Saxon bent his head affirmatively.

"So! a lumbering old box of pipes, only fit for firewood! What say you? Will you present the parish with a new one?"

"I hope the parish will not have to wait till I do so," replied Saxon, with a faint smile.

"But I am serious. Will you order one from Geneva, or have it brought all the way from Paris?"

"Cousin William, what *do* you mean?" faltered Saxon, his heart beginning to beat faster, he knew not why.

Mr. Trefalden laid his two hands on the young man's shoulders, and, looking him steadily in the face, replied:—

"This is what I mean, Saxon. In about a

fortnight's time you will be a rich man—a very rich man—ten times richer than Count Planta, or any nobleman here."

" I—rich—richer than——I do not understand you!" said Saxon, brokenly.

" It is the absolute truth."

" But my uncle——"

" He knows it. He has known it since before you were born. He has desired me to tell you all the story of your inheritance."

Saxon put his hand to his forehead, and turned his face away.

"Not just yet—not here," he said, in an agitated voice. "I—I am so taken by surprise —almost terrified. Will you leave me for a few minutes? I will come out to you presently in the churchyard."

" Oh, certainly," replied Mr. Trefalden, and turned towards the door. Saxon sprang after him, and grasped him by the arm.

" One moment," exclaimed he, pointing to a little stone tablet let into the church wall about half way between the organ and the porch. " Did *he* know, too ? "

The tablet bore the name of Saxon Trefalden, and the date of his death.

"Your father and your uncle both knew it," replied Mr. Trefalden, gravely. "This fortune would have been his now, instead of yours, if he had lived to claim it."

Saxon turned away with a deep sob, and his cousin went out into the sunshine.

Left alone in the little silent church, the young man covered his face with his hands, and burst into tears.

"God help me!" murmured he. "What shall I do? I am so young, so ignorant, so unfit to bear this burden. God help me, and guide me to use these riches rightly!"

And then he knelt down beside the little organ, and prayed.

CHAPTER XII.

A BROAD gravelled terrace lying due east and west, with vases of massive terra-cotta, full of glossy evergreens, placed at regular intervals along the verge of the broad parapet. A mighty old Elizabethan mansion of warm red brick, standing back in a deep angle of shade, with all its topmost gables, carved scutcheons, and gilded vanes glittering to the morning sun. A foreground of undulating park traversed by a noisy rivulet, and rich in old gnarled oaks planted at the time of the Restoration. A distance of blue hills and purple common, relieved here and there by stretches of fir plantation jutting out into the hazy heath-land, like wooded promontories sloping to the sea. On the terrace, a peacock with all his gorgeous plumage displayed; a lady

feeding him from her own white hand; and two
gentlemen standing by.   The time, the thirtieth
day of March, cool but sunny, and redolent
of spring.   The county, Surrey.   The place,
Castletowers.

"How you flatter that bird, Mademoiselle
Colonna!" said one of the gentlemen; a tall,
soldierly man, with a deep sabre-scar across his
left temple, and some few grey hairs silvering his
thick moustache and beard.   "His disposition
was always a perfect balance between vanity and
ill-nature, but since your advent, the brute has
become more insufferable than ever.   Take care!
I never see your hand so near his beak without a
shudder."

" Fear nothing on my account, Major Vaughan,"
replied the lady ; " and pray do not be unjust to
Sardanapalus.   He is quite an altered bird ; and
as gentle as a dove—with me."

" You do well to add that clause, my dear lady ;
for we can all bear witness to the way in which
his majesty 'takes it out' in viciousness when
you are not by.   He flew at Gulnare not an hour
ago, down by the five oaks yonder ; and I believe,

if I had not chanced to be within hail, and if the
mare were not the most self-possessed beast in
creation, there would have been battle, murder,
and sudden death between them."

"Really? You make me prouder than ever of
my conquest."

The soldier shrugged his shoulders.

"Pshaw!" said he, "what is one bar on the
medal, more or less, to the hero of a hundred
fields?"

"Major Vaughan, you are complimentary."

"Vaughan's pretty speeches always smell of
powder," laughed the younger gentleman, who
was leaning against the parapet close by.

"Bah! *que veux-tu, mon cher?* A man can
no more shake off the associations of twenty
years, than he can shake off the bronze from his
skin :—

> ' You may break, you may ruin the vase if you will,
> The scent of the *barrack* will hang round it still.' "

Mademoiselle Colonna looked up quickly, still
feeding the peacock from her open palm.

"I like your compliment the better, Major
Vaughan, for what Lord Castletowers calls its

smell of powder," said she.   "It is a familiar perfume to me, remember."

"I don't like to remember it," muttered the soldier, pulling thoughtfully at his moustache.

"Nor I," said Lord Castletowers, in a low voice.

"Why not, pray?" asked the lady, with a heightened colour.   "Is it not the incense of Italian liberty?"

"Granted; but it is an incense so powerful that fair ladies do well to smell it from a distance."

"Not when they can be of service in the temple, Major Vaughan," replied Mademoiselle Colonna, with one of her proud smiles.   "But, digressions apart, do you really tell me that Sardanapalus attacked Gulnare without any kind of provocation?"

"I do, indeed."

"It is strange that he should be so savage."

"It is still more strange that he should be so docile!   I believe, Mademoiselle Colonna, that you are in possession of some taming secret known only to yourself."

"Perhaps I am. May I be allowed to cite you as a specimen of my success?"

Major Vaughan bowed almost to the ground.

"Oh! daughter of the sun and moon," said he, "the head of thy slave is at thy disposal!"

Startled either by the Major's profound salaam, or by the sudden pealing of the breakfast bell, Sardanapalus threw up his head, and uttered an angry scream. Mademoiselle Colonna withdrew her hand quickly, and flung away the remainder of the cake with which she had been feeding him. Lord Castletowers saw the gesture, and sprang to her side.

"The brute has not bitten you?" he said anxiously.

She had already wrapped her handkerchief round her hand, and was moving slowly towards the house, as if nothing had happened; but there was a scarcely perceptible quiver in the smile with which she replied,

"Very slightly, thank you. Don't be angry with the poor bird. He meant no harm."

"Meant!" echoed the young man, fiercely. "I'll teach him to know what he means in future.

Will you permit me to see the extent of the mischief?"

"Nay, it is nothing—a mere peck."

Lord Castletowers uttered an exclamation of dismay, as he stooped to take something from the ground.   It was a little fragment of cake, all crimson dyed.

"It is no 'peck' that has done this!" he exclaimed.   "For pity's sake, Olim — mademoiselle, allow me to see your hand!"

"Indeed it is not serious; but lest you should fancy it worse than it is—there!"

The blush with which she began faded quite away as she concluded, and left her somewhat paler than usual.   She averted her eyes.   She could bear the pain bravely enough, but not the sight.

"What is the matter?" said Major Vaughan, who had turned away on making his salaam, and who had seen nothing of the accident.

"That carrion bird has bitten Mademoiselle Colonna!" replied Lord Castletowers, with unconcealed agitation.   "Bitten her severely.   See this!"

The pretty little delicate palm was half laid
open, but the slender fingers did not even
tremble. Major Vaughan examined the wound
with the keen glance of one accustomed to such
matters.

"Humph! an ugly gash!" said he; "but not
so bad as a bayonet thrust, after all. If you will
accompany me indoors, Miss Colonna, I will
dress it for you in first-rate style. You do not
know what a capital surgeon I am. Here,
Castletowers,——something to tie up the young
lady's hand, in the meanwhile!"

Lord Castletowers gave his own handkerchief,
and, turning aside, hastily thrust Mademoiselle
Colonna's into his breast-pocket. Her eyes were
still averted; but a dark shadow came upon
Major Vaughan's face.

"A thousand thanks," said she, smilingly,
when the bandage was adjusted.

"You must not thank me till it is properly
dressed," replied he, offering her his arm. "And
now, if you please, we will find our way to the
housekeeper's room, and procure all that is necessary; while you, my dear fellow, had better go

and explain the cause of this delay to Lady
Castletowers. I know she does not like to wait
for breakfast."

"True, it is one of my mother's peculiarities.
I will do the work of propitiation. As for
Sardanapalus . . . ."

"Sardanapalus must be pardoned," interposed
Mademoiselle Colonna.

Lord Castletowers shook his head.

"Nay, I entreat."

But she entreated with the air of an empress.

The young man lifted his hat.

"The prisoner at the bar was condemned to
death," said he, courteously; "but since the
queen chooses to exercise her prerogative, the
court commutes his sentence to solitary confine-
ment for life in the great aviary at the end of the
Italian garden."

At this moment the breakfast bell sent forth
a second clamorous peal; the imperial convict
uttered another dissonant cry, and sailed across
the terrace in all his panoply of plumage; and
the trio went up to the house.

CHAPTER XIII.

THE HOUSE OF CASTLETOWERS.

GERVASE LEOPOLD WYNNECLYFFE, Earl of Castletowers, was the fifth peer of his house, and the last of his name. He was not rich; but he was very good-natured. He had no great expectations: but he was tolerably clever, tolerably good-looking, and only twenty-seven years of age. His principles were sound; his French accent was perfect; he had made one successful speech in the House, and he was unmarried. With all these qualifications, and his five feet eleven inches to boot, it is not surprising that Lord Castletowers, despite his very limited means, should have found himself, during several seasons, the object of a fair amount of maternal manœuvring. That he was not yet given over to the spoilers was owing to no wisdom of his own,

and to no absence of that susceptibility which
flesh (especially flesh under thirty years of age) is
heir to. On the contrary, he had been smitten,
as the phrase goes, twice or thrice; but on each
of these occasions his destiny, and perhaps his
lady mother, had interposed to save him.

The young Earl adored his mother. She was
still beautiful; slender, pale, stately, and somewhat above the average height of women. In
complexion and features she resembled the later
portraits of Marie Antoinette; but it was a like-
ness of outline and colouring only. The expression was totally different—so different that it
appeared sometimes to obliterate the resemblance
altogether. The sorrow, the sweetness, the
womanly tenderness of that poor royal face
were all missing from the serene countenance of
Alethea, Countess of Castletowers. She looked
as if she had never known a strong emotion in
her life; as if love and hate, anguish and terror,
would have glanced off from her like arrows from
a marble statue. Proud as they both were, the
very pride of these two faces had nothing in
common. That of the queen was passionate,

upon the lip; that of the countess shone coldly
from the eye.   Pride was, indeed, the dominant
principle of her being—the pivot upon which
her every thought, word, and action turned.   She
had been a great heiress.   She was the daughter,
wife, and mother of an Earl.   She was of the
ancient line of Holme-Pierrepoint; and the blood
of the Holme-Pierrepoints had mingled once with
that of the Plantagenets, and twice with that
of the Tudors.   The Countess of Castletowers
never forgot these things for a moment.   It is
doubtful if they were even absent from her
dreams.   Her dignity, her grace, her suavity of
manner were perfect; but they were all based
upon her pride, like that royal bower of which
the poet dreamed :—

"A sunny pleasure-dome, with caves of ice."

Lady Castletowers had not loved her husband;
but she loved her son as much as it was in her
nature to love anything.   The husband had
squandered her dowry; insulted her by open
neglect; and died abroad, overwhelmed with
debt and discredit, within the fifth year of their

marriage. The son had reverenced, admired, idolised her from his cradle. He had never given her cause for one moment's anxiety since the day of his birth. As a little child, he thought her the most noble and gracious of God's crea‑ tures: as he grew in years, his faith in her remained undiminished, and his love became that beautiful love which mingles the chivalrous re‑ spect of the man with the tender homage of the son. It was not, therefore, surprising that what‑ ever waif of human weakness had fallen to her ladyship's portion should have been garnered up for this one object. While he was yet very young, her affection for him was, as it were, invested at compound interest, and left to accu‑ mulate till he should become of an age to deserve it; but as he arrived at manhood, his life became identified with her own. All her pride and am‑ bition centred in him. He must marry well— that is to say, richly and nobly. He must make a position in the Upper House. He must some day be a cabinet minister; and he must get that step in the peerage which the Duke of York had once solicited for his father, but which George

the Fourth had refused to grant. Lady Castletowers had set her heart on obtaining these
things for her son, but above all else had she
set her heart upon the last.   She would have
sold ten years of her own life to see the marquis's
coronet upon his carriage panels.   When the
clergyman in church put up that prayer, towards
the end of the morning service, which implores
fulfilment for the desires and petitions of the
congregation, " as may be most expedient for
them," Lady Castletowers invariably reverted in
the silence of her thoughts to the four pearls
and the four strawberry leaves; and never
asked herself if there could be profanity in the
prayer.

In the meanwhile, the young Earl accepted all
this pride and ambition for the purest maternal
affection.   He did not care in the least about
the marquisate ; he was somewhat indifferent to
the attractions of the Upper House ; and he had
almost made up his mind that he would not, if
he could, be burdened with the toils and respon-
sibilities of office. But he would not have grieved
his mother by a hint of these heresies, for the

universe. He even blamed himself for his own
want of ambition, and soothed his troubled con-
science every now and then by promising himself
that he would very soon "read up" one of the
popular financial topics, and make another speech
in the House.

But that question of the wealthy marriage was
to him the least agreeable of all his mother's
projects. There was some romance in the young
man's disposition, and he could not relish the
thought of adding to his own scanty acres by
means of his wife's fortune. He would have preferred to marry a village maiden for love, like the
Lord of Burleigh ; or, at least, to have felt that
he was free to love like the Lord of Burleigh, if
he chose.

It was in somewhat of this same spirit of
romance that Lord Castletowers had associated
himself with the Italian cause. He had, or fancied that he had, a democratic bias. He was
fond of quoting the examples of the classic repub-
lics ; he had read Rousseau's " *Contrat Social*,"
and Godwin's " Political Justice ; " and he had a
genuine English hatred of oppression, whatever

its form or aspect. Surrounded as he had been since the hour of his birth by a triple rampart of conservatism, it is possible that democracy possessed for this young nobleman somewhat of the stimulative charm of a forbidden luxury. He certainly never confided the full extent of his republican sympathies to his lady mother, and he would have been far from grateful to any officious friend who had presented her with a verbatim report of certain of his most enthusiastic speeches. Those speeches were delivered at meetings held in obscure lecture-halls and institutes in unaristocratic parts of London, and were remarkably good speeches of their kind—vigorously thought, and often felicitously expressed; but their eloquence, nevertheless, was by no means calculated to gratify the Countess of Castletowers.

On all questions of English polity, Lord Castletowers was what is somewhat vaguely called a "liberal conservative;" on all Italian subjects, a thorough-going *bonnet rouge*. He would no more have advocated universal suffrage in his own country than he would have countenanced slavery in Venetia; but he firmly believed in the possible regeneration of the great Roman republic, and avowed that belief with unhesitating enthusiasm. Besides, his old college tastes and associations were yet fresh upon him, and he entertained all a young man's admiration for the Latin heroes, poets, and historians. Nor were his sympathies all so classical and remote. He was keenly susceptible to those influences which beset the travelled amateur of books and art. He had loitered, sketched, and dreamed away more than one winter among the palaces of Florence and Rome. He had read Petrarch, and Tasso, and the most amusing parts of Dante. He had been in love, though never, perhaps, very deeply, with scores of dark-eyed Giuliettas and Biancas. He had written canzonets in which *amore* rhymed to *core* in the orthodox fashion, and had sung them by moonlight under picturesque balconies, over and over again, in many a stately old Italian city. Above all, he had known Giulio Colonna from his earliest boyhood, and had been, as it were, inoculated with Italian patriotism ere he knew what patriotism meant.

Accustomed to regard Signor Colonna not only
as some kind of distant cousin, but also as one
of his mother's most frequent guests, he had
accepted all his opinions with the unquestioning
faith of childhood. He had, indeed, listened to
the magic of his eloquence long before he was of
an age to understand its force and purport, and
had become insensibly educated in the love and
reverence of those things which were to Giulio
Colonna as the life of his life. It was, therefore,
no wonder that the young Earl proved, as he
grew to man's estate, a staunch friend to the
Italian cause. It was no wonder that he made
enthusiastic speeches at obscure meetings, trans-
acted a vast amount of really hard work in his
capacity of Honorary Secretary to the Central
Committee, and believed in Giulio Colonna and
the great Italian republic of the future, with all
his heart and soul.

There was, in reality, no blood relationship
whatever between the Castletowers family and
this branch of the Colonnas. A Miss Holme-
Pierrepoint had married a Prince Colonna some
sixty-five or seventy years before; but of this

marriage no children had been born. A pleasant intercourse had subsisted, however, between
the two families ever since. The Colonnas,
down to the third and fourth generation, were
royally welcomed at the grand old Surrey mansion, whenever any of them came to England.
Lady Castletowers and her son had once spent
six delightful weeks of villegiatura at Prince
Colonna's Alban Villa; and when the young
Earl was in Rome, he had been the very life and
soul of all the winter entertainments given at
that stately palazzo which stands in the Corso at
the corner of the Piazza di Santissimi Apostoli.
As for Giulio Colonna, he had been *l'intime du
maison* ever since the Honourable Alethea Pierrepoint had exchanged her name for that of Castletowers—just as he had been *l'intime du maison*
at the house of her ladyship's father. He was
one of the very few whom the countess really
valued, and whom she condescended to call by
the sacred name of friend. Perhaps he was the
only person upon earth who could be said to
enjoy her ladyship's confidence. It was to him
that she had turned for help in her matrimonial

troubles; for advice respecting the education of her son; for sympathy when any of her ambitious projects failed of success. She had known him, indeed, from her girlhood. She admired his great and varied talents; she had perfect reliance on his probity and honour; and she respected his nobility of birth. To a certain extent she respected his patriotic devotion as well; though, it is almost needless to add, she was wholly at issue with him on the subject of republicanism.

"It is a point," she used to observe, " upon which my good friend, Signor Colonna, is deaf, I grieve to say, alike to reason and good taste. He has so imbued himself with the classical history of his country, that he can no longer discriminate between the necessities of a semi-barbarous race and those of a highly civilised people. He cannot see that the monarchical form of government is precisely that which the age demands. I am very sorry for him. I have represented the matter to him, over and over again, from every conceivable point of view; but with unvarying ill success. I am weary of trying to convince a man who shuts his ears to conviction."

And when she had said this, or words to this effect, Lady Castletowers would sigh, and drop the subject with the air of one who had exhausted it utterly.

CHAPTER XIV.

MOTHER AND SON.

"LATE, and alone, Gervase?" said Lady Castle-towers, with cold displeasure. "The breakfast bell rang ten minutes ago. Where are our guests?"

"I am sorry to have kept you waiting, mother," replied the Earl, "and you will be sorry for the cause. Sardanapalus has bitten Miss Colonna in the hand, and Vaughan has gone round with her to Mrs. Walker's room to get it dressed. I always said that confounded bird would do mischief some day. Where's Colonna?"

"In his room, I suppose, and deaf, as usual, to the bell. Is Olimpia much hurt?"

"Painfully; but of course not dangerously."

"There is no necessity for my presence?"

"No absolute necessity," rejoined the young

Earl, with some hesitation, and a little emphasis.

The Countess seated herself at the breakfast table, and dismissed the servant in attendance.

"I am glad," said she, "of a few moments alone with you, Gervase. How long does Major Vaughan propose to remain with us?"

"I really do not know. He has said nothing about it, and I fancy his time just now is at his own disposal."

"I think we ought to do something to make Castletowers pleasant to him while he is here."

"I was intending to make the same remark to you, my dear mother," replied the young man. "I have, indeed, asked some men from town, and I rather think Charley Burgoyne and Edward Brandon may be down next week; but, that is not enough. Shall we give a ball?"

"Or a fête—but perhaps the season is hardly sufficiently advanced for a fête at present."

"And then a fête is so confoundedly expensive!" groaned the Earl. "It won't be so bad after the half-yearly rents have come in; but I assure you, mother, I was shocked when I looked

into my banker's book yesterday. We have
barely a couple of hundreds to carry us through
up to Midsummer!"

The Countess sighed, and tapped impatiently
on the edge of the. table with her delicate,
jewelled fingers.

" It's a miserable thing to be poor !" ejaculated
the Earl.

" My poor boy, it is indeed ! "

" If it hadn't been for selling those two
farms . . . "

" In order to pay off the mortgage which your
father's extravagance entailed upon us !" interrupted Lady Castletowers, bitterly.

" If it hadn't been for paying that off," he
continued, " our means would now have been so
comfortable ! That twenty-five thousand pounds,
mother, would have made us rich."

" Comparatively rich," replied the Countess.

" Well, it's of no use to be always moaning,
like the harbour bar in Kingsley's poem," said
the young man, with an air of forced gaiety.
" We *are* poor, dearest mother, and we must
make the best of it. In the meanwhile, let us,

by all means, give some kind of entertainment.
You can think the matter over, and whatever you
decide upon is sure to be best and wisest. I
must find the money, somehow. Perhaps Trefalden could advance me a hundred or two."

" Has he not lately come into an enormous
fortune ? " asked the Countess, abstractedly.

" No, not our Trefalden, but some member, I
believe, of his family. I don't know the story,
but I have heard it is something very romantic.
However, Trefalden himself is a rich man—he's
too quiet and clever not to be rich. At all events,
I can but ask him."

" I don't like you to borrow money, Gervase,"
said Lady Castletowers.

" I abhor it, in the ordinary sense of the word,'
replied her son. " But a gentleman may draw
upon his lawyer for a small sum without scruple.
It is not at all the same thing."

" If I could but see you well married ! " sighed
the Countess.

Lord Castletowers shrugged his shoulders.

" And occupying that position in the country
to which your birth and talents entitle you ! I

was talking about you the other day to the Duke
of Dorchester. He seems to think there must be
a change in the ministry before long; and then,
if he, and one or two others of our acquaintance,
get into office—*nous verrons!*"

"There are always so many ifs," said Lord
Castletowers, with a smile.

"By the way, Miss Hatherton—the rich Miss
Hatherton—is staying at Aylsham Park. Of
course, if we give a fête, the Walkingshaws will
bring her with them. It is said, Gervase, that
she has two hundred and fifty thousand pounds."

"Indeed!" said Lord Castletowers, indiffe-
rently.

"And she is handsome."

"Yes—she is handsome."

The Countess looked at her son. The Earl
looked out of the window.

"I fancy," said the Countess, "that Major
Vaughan is paying a good deal of attention to
Olimpia."

"To—to Miss Colonna!" said the Earl, with
an involuntary catching of his breath. "Impossible!"

" Why impossible ? "

" Because——Well, perhaps I scarcely know why; but it seems so unlikely."

" Why unlikely ? " pursued the Countess, coldly and steadily.

" Well—Vaughan is not a marrying man—and he has no private means, or next to none, besides his pay—and—and then, they are so utterly unsuited—unsuited in every way—in tastes, ages, dispositions, everything ! "

The young man spoke hastily, and with a perceptibly heightened colour. His mother, still coldly observing him, went on.

" I do not agree with you, Gervase," said she, " in any one of your objections. I believe that Major Vaughan would quite willingly marry, if Olimpia were the lady. He is not more than forty; and if he has only a few hundreds a year besides his pay, he is, at all events, richer than Olimpia's father. Besides, he is a gallant officer; and if all that Colonna anticipates should come to pass, a gallant officer would be worth more than a mere fortune, just now, to the Italian cause."

The Earl still stood by the window, looking out at the park and the blue hills far away; but made no reply.

" He has said nothing to you upon the sub-ject?" said Lady Castletowers.

" Nothing."

" Perhaps, however, it is hardly likely that he would do so."

" Most unlikely, I should say.   But here's the letter-bag—and here come surgeon and patient."

Lady Castletowers became at once condolent and sympathetic; Mademoiselle Colonna laughed off the accident with impatient indifference; Major Vaughan bowed over his hostess's fair hand; and all took their places at table.

" A budget, as usual, for Colonna," said Lord Castletowers, sorting the pile of letters just tumbled out of the bag.   " One, two, three billets, redolent of what might be called the parfum du boudoir, for Vaughan—also, as usual!   Two letters, my dearest mother, for you; and only one (a square-shouldered, round-fisted, blue-com-plexioned, obstinate-looking business document) for myself.   A pretty thing to lie at the bottom of one's letter bag, like hope at the bottom of Pandora's casket!"

"It hath a Bond Street aspect, Castletowers, that affects me unpleasantly," said Major Vaughan, from whose brow the angry flush with which he had received his three letters and swept them carelessly on one side, had not yet quite faded.

"Say rather a Chancery Lane aspect," replied the young Earl, breaking the seal as he spoke; "and that's as much worse than Bond Street as Newgate is worse than the Queen's Bench."

"Bond Street and Chancery Lane, Newgate and the Queen's Bench!" repeated Mademoiselle Colonna. "The conversation sounds very awful. What does it all mean?"

"I presume," said Lady Castletowers, "that Major Vaughan supposed the letter to be written by a—a tailor, or some person of that description; while it really comes from my son's lawyer, Mr. Trefalden."

"I met Mr. Trefalden a few weeks ago," said Mademoiselle Colonna, "in Switzerland."

"In Switzerland?" echoed Lord Castletowers.

"And he authorised me to add his name to our general committee list."

"A miracle! a miracle!"

"And why a miracle?" asked Lady Castletowers. "Does Mr. Trefalden disapprove of the Italian cause?"

"Mr. Trefalden, my dear mother, never approves or disapproves of any public movement whatever. Nature seems to have created him without opinions."

"Then he is either a very superficial or a very ambitious man," said Lady Castletowers.

"The latter, depend on it. He's a remarkably clever fellow, and has good interest, no doubt. He will set his politics to the tune of his interest some day, and make his way to the woolsack 'in a galliard.'"

"I am glad this is but a conjectural estimate of Mr. Trefalden's character," said Olimpia.

"You like him, then?" said Major Vaughan, hastily.

"I neither like him nor dislike him; but if these were proven facts, I could never speak to him again."

Signor Colonna came in and made his morning salutations, his eyes wandering eagerly towards his letters all the time.

"Good morning—good morning. Late, did you say? *Peccavi!* So I am. I lost myself in the library. Bell! I heard no bell. Pray forgive me, dear Lady Castletowers. Any news to-day? You were early this morning, Major Vaughan. Saw you in the saddle soon after six. Plenty of letters this morning, I see—plenty of letters!"

And with this he slipped into his seat, and became at once immersed in the contents of the documents before him.

"Trefalden writes from town, mother," said Lord Castletowers. "He excuses his delay on the plea of much business. He has been settling his cousin's affairs—the said cousin having come in for between four and five millions sterling."

"A man who comes in for four or five millions sterling has no right to live," said Major Vaughan. "His very being is an insult to his offended species."

"But if this cousin should prove to be a lady?" suggested Mademoiselle Colonna.

"I would condemn her, of course—to matrimony."

"I should think Trefalden would take care of that!" laughed the Earl.

"But *is* the cousin a lady?" asked Lady Castletowers, with seeming indifference.

"Alas! no, my dear mother: too surely he belongeth to the genus homo. Trefalden's words are—'I have been assisting my cousin in the arrangement of his affairs, he having lately inherited a fortune of between four and five millions sterling.'"

"I have no doubt that he is fat, ugly, and disagreeable," said Major Vaughan.

"And plebeian," added Lady Castletowers, with a smile.

"And illiberal," said Olimpia.

"And, in short, so rich," said the Earl, "that were he hideous and ignorant as Caliban, society would receive him with open arms, and the beauty of the season would gladly wear orange-blossoms for him at St. George's! What says

this honourable company—shall I invite him
down to Castletowers for a week or two, and shall
we all fall to worshipping the golden calf?"

"Not for the world!" exclaimed Olimpia,
scornfully; but she was the only one who replied.

The breakfast party then broke up. The Earl
went to his stables, Olimpia to her apartments,
and Major Vaughan to the billiard-room. Signor
Colonna and Lady Castletowers strolled to and
fro in the sunshine, outside the breakfast-room
windows.

"But who is this millionaire?" asked the
Italian, eagerly.

"*Caro amico*, you know as much as I know,"
replied Lady Castletowers. "He is a cousin of
our solicitor, Mr. Trefalden, who is a very well-
bred gentlemanly person. As for this fortune,
I think I have heard that it has been accumulating for one or two centuries—but that is probably a mere rumour."

"Between four and five millions!" ejaculated
Colonna. "With such a fortune, what might
not be done by a friend to the cause!"

Lady Castletowers smiled.

"*Sempre Italia!*" she said.

"*Sempre Italia!*" replied he, lifting his hat reverently as he pronounced the words. "While I live, Lady Castletowers. While I live."

They had come now to the end of the path, and were about to return, when he laid his hand on hers, and said, very earnestly—

"I wish I could see this man. I wish I knew him. I have won over thousands of recruits in my time, Alethea—thousands, who had only their blood to give, and gave it. Money is as precious as blood in a cause like ours. If we had had but *one* million, eighteen months ago, Italy would now have been free."

"Ah, you want me to help you—you want Gervase to bring him here? Is that so?"

"Precisely."

"Well, I suppose it can be done—somehow."

"I think it can," replied Colonna. "I am sure it can."

"And it might lead to great results, eh?"

"It might, indeed it might."

"Your personal influence, I know, is almost

magical," mused Lady Castletowers; "and if our millionaire should prove to be young and impressionable. . . ."

She hesitated. He looked up, and their eyes met.

"Olimpia is very lovely," she said, smiling; "and very fascinating."

"I have thought of that," he replied. "I have thought of that; and Olimpia would never marry any man who did not devote himself to Italy, body and soul!"

"And purse," added Lady Castletowers, quietly.

"And purse—of course," said he, with a somewhat heightened colour.

"Then I will do what I can, dear old friend, for your sake," said Lady Castletowers, affectionately.

"And I," he replied, "will do what I can for the sake of the cause. God knows, Alethea, that I do it for the cause alone—God knows how pure my soul is of any other aim or end!"

"I am sure of it," she replied, abstractedly.

"Had I but the half of four or five millions

at command, the stake upon which I have set
my whole life, and my child's life, would be won.
Do you hear me, Alethea? would be, *must* be
won!"

"And shall be won, *amico,* if any help of mine
can avail you," said Lady Castletowers. "I will
speak to Gervase about it at once. He shall ask
both the cousins down."

"Best friend," murmured the Italian, taking
the hand which she extended to him, and pressing
it gratefully in both his own.

"But beware!—not a word to him of all this.
He has his English notions of hospitality—*tu
comprends?*"

"Yes—it is true."

"Adieu, then, till luncheon."

"Addio."

And the Countess, with a look of unusual pre-
occupation on her fair brow, went slowly back
to the house, thinking of many things: chiefly
of how her son should some day marry an
heiress, and how Olimpia Colonna should be
disposed of to Saxon Trefalden.

CHAPTER XV.

A TALL young man stood at the first floor window of a fashionable hotel in Piccadilly, drumming upon the plate-glass panes, and staring listlessly down upon the crowded street below. It was about two o'clock in the day, and the brilliant thoroughfare was all alive with colour and sunshine; but his face took no joyousness from the busy scene. It wore, on the contrary, as gloomy and discontented an expression as such a bright young face could well put on. The ceaseless ebb and flow of gorgeous equipages; the fair pedestrians in their fashionable toilettes, even the little band of household troops riding by in helm and cuirass, failed apparently to interest that weary spectator. He yawned, looked at his watch, took an im-

patient turn or two about the room, and then
went back to the window, and drummed again
upon the panes. Some books, an opera glass,
and one or two newspapers lay on the table;
but the leaves of the books were uncut, and
only one of the newspapers had been unfolded.
Too *ennuyé* to read, and too restless to sit still,
this young man evidently found his time hang
heavily upon his hands.

Presently a cab drove up to the hotel, and two
gentlemen jumped out. The first of these was
William Trefalden; the second, Lord Castletowers. William Trefalden looked up and
nodded, as he came up the broad stone steps,
and the watcher at the window ran joyously to
meet him on the stairs.

"I'm so glad you're come!" was his eager
exclamation. "I've been watching for you, and
the time has seemed so long!"

"I am only twenty minutes late," replied
Mr. Trefalden, smiling.

"But it's so dreary here!"

"And I bring you a visitor," continued the
other. "Lord Castletowers, allow me to present

my cousin, Mr. Saxon Trefalden. Saxon, Lord Castletowers is so kind as to desire your acquaintance."

Saxon put out his hand, and gave the Earl's a hearty shake. He would as soon have thought of greeting his guest with a bow as of flinging him over the balcony into the street below.

"Thank you," said he. "I'm very much obliged to you."

"I am surprised that you find this situation 'dreary,' Mr. Trefalden," said Lord Castletowers, with a glance towards the window.

"I find all London dreary," replied Saxon, bluntly.

"May I ask how long you have been here?"

"About a week."

"Then you have really had no time to form an opinion."

"I have had time to be very miserable," said Saxon. "I never was so miserable in my life. The noise and hurry of London bewilder me. I can settle to nothing. I can think of nothing. I can do nothing. I find it impossible to read ; and if I go out alone in the streets, I lose myself.

Then there seems to be no air. I have inhaled smoke and dust, but I have not *breathed* since I came into the place."

"Your first impressions of our Babel are certainly not *couleur de rose*," said the Earl laughingly.

"They are *couleur de* Lothbury, and *couleur de* Chancery Lane," interposed William Trefalden. "My cousin, Lord Castletowers, has for the last ten days been the victim of the law. We have been putting him in possession of his property, and he has seen nothing of town save the gold regions East of Temple Bar."

"An excellent beginning," said the Earl. "The finest pass into Belgravia is through Threadneedle Street."

"And the noblest prospect in London is the Bank of England," added the lawyer.

"I thought it very ugly and dirty," said Saxon innocently.

"I hope this law business is all over now," said Lord Castletowers.

"Yes, for the present; and Saxon has nothing to do but to amuse himself."

"Amuse myself!" echoed Saxon. "I must go home to do that."

"Because Reichenau is so gay, or because you find London so uninviting?" asked the Earl, with a smile.

"Because I am a born mountaineer, and because to me this place is a prison. I must have air to breathe, hills to climb, and a gun on my shoulder. *That* is what I call amusement."

"That is what I call amusement also," said Lord Castletowers; "and if you will come down to Surrey, I can give you plenty of it—a fishing-rod, and a hunter included. But in the meanwhile, you must let us prove to you that London is not so barren of entertainment as you seem to think."

"Let this help to prove it," said Mr. Trefalden, taking from his pocket a little oblong book in a green paper cover. "There's magic in these pages, my dear fellow. They contain all the wit, wisdom, and beauty of the world we live in. While you have this in your pocket, you will never want for amusement—or friends; and when you have come to the end of the present volume, the publishers will furnish you with another."

"What is it?" said Saxon, turning it over somewhat doubtfully.

"A cheque-book."

"Pshaw! money again—always money!"

"Don't speak of it disrespectfully. You have more than you can count, and as yet you neither know what it is worth, nor what to do with it."

"Pray enlighten me, then," said Saxon, with a touch of impatience in his voice. "Tell me, in the first place, what it *is* worth?"

"That is a matter of individual opinion," replied Mr. Trefalden, with one of his quiet smiles. "If you ask Lord Castletowers, he will probably tell you that it is worth less than noble blood, bright eyes, or Italian liberty. If you ask a plodding fellow like myself, he will probably value it above all three."

"Well then, in the second place, what am I to do with it?"

"Spend it."

Saxon shrugged his shoulders; and Lord Castletowers, who had coloured up somewhat

angrily the minute before, laughed, and said that
it was good advice.

"Spend it," repeated the lawyer. " You never
will know how to employ your money till you
acquire the art of getting rid of it. You have yet
to learn that instead of turning every thing into
gold, like Midas, you can turn gold into everything. It is the true secret of the transmutation
of metal."

"Shall I be any the wiser or happier for this
knowledge?" asked Saxon, with a sigh.

"You cannot help being the wiser," laughed
his cousin; "nor, I should think, the happier.
You will cease to be 'dreary' in the first place.
He who has plenty of money, and knows how to
spend it, is never in want of entertainment."

"Ay, 'and knows how'! There is my difficulty."

"If you had read Molière," replied Mr. Trefalden, "you would be aware that a rich man has
discernment in his purse."

"Cousin, you are laughing at me."

It was said with perfect good humour, but
with such directness that even Mr. Trefalden's

practised self-possession was momentarily troubled.

"But I suppose you think a rich fellow can
afford to be laughed at," added Saxon, "and I
am quite of your opinion. It will help to civilise
me, and that, you know, is your mission. And
now for a lesson in alchemy. What shall I transmute my gold into first?"

"Nay, into whatever seems to you to be best
worth the trouble," replied Mr. Trefalden. "First
of all, I should say, into a certain amount of
superfine Saxony and other cloths; into a large
stock of French kid and French cambric—and a
valet. After that—well, after that, suppose you
ask Lord Castletowers' opinion."

"I vote for a tall horse, a short tiger, and a
cab," said the young Earl.

"And chambers in St. James's Street," suggested the lawyer.

"And a stall at Gye's."

"And all the flowers, pictures, Baskerville
editions, Delphin classics, organs, and Etruscan
antiquities you take it into your head to desire!
That's the way to transmute your metal, you

happy fellow!   Taken as a philosophical experiment, I know nothing more beautiful, simple, and satisfactory."

"You bewilder me," said poor Saxon.   "You speak a language which is partly jest and partly earnest, and I know not where the earnestness ends, or where the jest begins.   What is it that you really mean?   I am quite willing to do what you conceive a man in my position should do; but you must show me how to set about it."

"I am here to-day for no other purpose."

"And more than this, you must give me leave to reject your system, if I dislike, or grow weary of it."

"What! return to roots and woad after Kühn and Stultz?"

"Certainly, if I find the roots more palatable, and the woad more becoming."

"Agreed.   Then we begin at once.   You shall put yourself under my guidance, and that of Lord Castletowers.   You shall obey us implicitly for the next six or eight hours, and you shall begin by writing a cheque for five hundred, which we can cash at Drummond's as we go along."

"With all my heart," said Saxon; and so, aided by his cousin's instructions, sat down and wrote his first cheque.

"He's a capital fellow," said Lord Castletowers to Mr. Trefalden, as they went down the hotel stairs; "a splendid fellow, and I like him thoroughly. Shall I propose him at the Erectheum? He ought to belong to a club, and I know some men there who would be delighted to do what they could for any member of my introduction."

"By all means. It is the very thing for him," replied Mr. Trefalden. "He must have acquaintances, you know; and it is out of the question that a busy man like myself should do the honours of town to him, or anyone. Were he my own brother, I would not undertake it."

"And I am never here myself for many days at a time," said the Earl. "London is an expensive luxury, and I am obliged to make a little of it go a long way. However, while I am here, and whenever I am here, it will give me a great deal of pleasure to show Mr. Saxon Trefalden any attention in my power."

"You are very kind. Saxon, my dear fellow,

Lord Castletowers is so good as to offer to get you into the Erectheum."

"The Erectheum of Athens?" exclaimed Saxon, opening his blue eyes in laughing astonishment.

"Nonsense—of Pall Mall. It is a fashionable club."

"I am much obliged to Lord Castletowers," replied Saxon, vaguely. But he had no more notion of the nature, objects, or aims of a fashionable club than a Bedouin Arab.

CHAPTER XVI.

THE ERECTHEUM.

"No, by Jove, Brandon, not a bit of a snob! As green as an Arcadian, but no more of a snob than——"

Sir Charles Burgoyne was going to say, "than you are;" but he changed his mind, and said, instead :—

"—than Castletowers himself."

"I call any man a snob who quotes Bion and Moschus in his familiar talk," replied the other, all unconscious of his friend's hesitation. "How the deuce is one to remember anything about Bion and Moschus? and what right has he to make a fellow look like a fool?"

"Unfeeling, I admit," replied Sir Charles, languidly.

"I hate your learned people," said Brandon,

irritably. "And I hate parvenus. Ignorant parvenus are bad enough; but learned parvenus are the worst of all. He's both—hang him!"

"Hang him, by all means!" said another young man, approaching the window at which the two were standing. "May I ask who he is, and what he has done?"

It was in one of the princely reading-rooms of the Erectheum Club, Pall Mall. The two first speakers were the Honourable Edward Brandon, third and youngest son of Hardicanute, fourteenth Earl of Ipswich, and Sir Charles Burgoyne, Baronet, of the Second Life Guards.

There are men whom nature seems to have run up by contract, and the Honourable Edward Brandon was one of them. He was just like one of those slight, unsubstantial, fashionable houses that spring up every day like mushrooms about Bayswater and South Kensington, and are hired under the express condition of never being danced in. He was very young, very tall, and as economically supplied with brain and muscle as a man could well be. The very smallest appreciable weight of knowledge would have broken down his understanding at any moment; and his little ornaments of manner were all in the flimsiest modern taste, and of the merest stucco. He "dipped" occasionally into "Bell's Life" and the "Court Circular." He had read half of the first volume of "Mr. Soapey Sponge's Sporting Tour." He played croquet pretty well, and billiards very badly, and was saturated through and through with smoke, like a Finnan haddock.

Sir Charles Burgoyne was a man of a very different stamp. He was essentially one of a class; but then, ethnologically speaking, his class was many degrees higher than that of Mr. Brandon. He was better built, and better furnished. He rode well; was a good shot; played a first-rate game at billiards; was gifted with a certain lazy impertinence of speech and manner that passed for wit; and was so effeminately fair of complexion and regular of feature, that he was popularly known among his brother officers as "The Beauty."

The last comer — short, sallow, keen-eyed, somewhat flippant in his address, and showy in his attire—was Laurence Greatorex, Esquire,

only son, heir, and partner of Sir Samuel Greatorex, Knight, the well-known banker and alderman of Lombard Street, City.

"Hang him, by all means!" said this gentleman, with charming impartiality. "Who is he?
and what has he done?"

"We were speaking of the new member,"
replied Brandon.

"What, Crœsus Trefalden? Pshaw! The
man's an outer barbarian. What social enor-
mity has he been committing now?"

"He's been offending Brandon's delicate sense
of propriety by quoting Greek," said The Beauty.

"Greek! Unpardonable offence! What shall
we do to him? Muzzle him?"

"Condemn him to feed on Greek roots for the
term of his natural life, like Timon of Athens,"
suggested the Beauty, lazily.

"He's little better than a savage as it is,"
said Mr. Greatorex, with a contemptuous shrug
of the shoulders. "He knows nothing of life,
and cares nothing for it, either. Last Tuesday,
when all the fellows were wild about the great
fight down at Barney's Croft, he sat and read

Homer, as if it were the news of the day.   He's
an animated anachronism—that's what he is, Sir
Charles."

"Who the deuce is he?" ejaculated Brandon.
"Where does he come from?"

"Heaven knows!   His father was a black
letter folio, I believe, and his mother a palimp-
sest."

"You're too witty to-day, Mr. Greatorex,"
sneered Burgoyne.

"Then he's so offensively rich!   Why, he put
down a thousand yesterday for Willis's subscrip-
tion!   There's his name at the head of the list!
Makes us look rather small—eh?"

"Confound his assurance!" broke out Brandon.   "He's not been here much more than a
week!   What's Willis to him, that he should
give more than the oldest members of the
club?"

"Well, it's a munificent donation," said the
Guardsman, good-naturedly.

"Munificent?   Hang his munificence!   I
suppose the members of the Erectheum can
pension off a secretary, who has served them for

fifteen years, without the help of a thousand pounds from a puppy like that!"

"Your virtuous indignation, Brandon, is quite refreshing," said Burgoyne. "How long have *you* been here, for instance? Half a year?"

"It was in bad taste, anyhow," said Greatorex; "deuced bad taste. It's always the way with your *nouveaux riches*. A man who had been wealthy all his life would have known better."

"Yourself, *par exemple*," retorted the Guardsman, insolently.

"Just so, Sir Charles; but then I'm to the money-market born, so hardly a case in point."

"Where did this Trefalden get his fortune?" asked Brandon. "I've heard that some fellow left it to him a hundred years ago, and that it has been accumulating ever since; but that's nonsense, of course."

"Sounds like a pecuniary version of the 'Sleeping Beauty,'" observed the baronet, parenthetically.

"I know no more than you do Mr. Brandon," replied Greatorex. "I *have* heard only the

common story of how this money has been lying
at compound interest for a century or more, and
has devolved to our pre-Adamite friend at last,
bringing him as many millions as he has fingers.
Some say double that sum ; but ten are enough
for my credulity."

"Does he bank with Sir Samuel?" asked
Brandon.

"No. Our shop lies too far east for him, I
suspect. He has opened an account at Drummond's. By the way, Sir Charles, what have
you decided upon doing with that brown mare of
yours? You seemed half inclined to part from
her a few days ago."

"You mean the Lady of Lyons?"

"I do."

"Sold her, Mr. Greatorex."

"Sold her, Sir Charles?"

"Yes—cab and all."

The banker turned very red, and bit his
lip.

"Would it be a liberty to ask the name of the
purchaser?" said he.

"Perhaps it would," replied the Guardsman.

"But I don't mind telling you. It's Mr. Trc-falden."

"Trefalden! Then, upon my soul, Sir Charles, it's too bad! I'm sorry to hear it. I am, indeed. I had hoped—in fact, I had expected—upon my soul, I had expected, Sir Charles, that you would have given me the opportunity. Money would have been no object. I would have given a fancy price for that mare with pleasure."

"Thank you, I did not want a fancy price," replied the Guardsman, haughtily.

"Besides, if you'll excuse me, Sir Charles, I must say I don't think it was quite fair, either."

"Fair?" echoed Burgoyne. "Really, Mr. Greatorex, I do not apprehend your meaning."

"Well, you know, Sir Charles, I spoke first; and as for Crœsus Trefalden, who scarcely knows a horse from a buffalo. . . . ."

"Mr. Saxon Trefalden is the friend of Lord Castletowers," interrupted Burgoyne, still more haughtily, "and I was very happy to oblige him."

If Sir Charles Burgoyne had not been a

baronet, a Guardsman, and a member of the
Erectheum club, it is possible that Mr. Greatorex
of Lombard Street would have given him the re-
tort uncourteous; but as matters stood, he only
grew a little redder; looked at his watch in
some confusion; and prudently swallowed his
annoyance.

"Oh, of course—in that case," stammered he,
"Lord Castletowers being your friend, I have
nothing more to say. Do you go down to his
place in Surrey next week, by-the-by?"

"Do *you?*" said Burgoyne, smoothing his
flaxen moustache, and looking down at the small
city man with half-closed eyes.

"I hope so, since his lordship has been kind
enough to invite me; but we are so deucedly
busy in Lombard Street just now that . . . .
pshaw! twelve o'clock already, and I am due in
the city at twenty minutes past. Not a moment
to lose. 'I know a bank,' *et cætera*—but there's
no wild time there for anybody between twelve
and three! Good morning, Mr. Brandon. Good
morning, Sir Charles."

The baronet bent his head about a quarter of

an inch, and almost before the other was out of
hearing, said :—

" That man is *bourgeois* to the tips of his
fingers, and insufferably familiar. Why do you
tolerate him, Brandon ? "

" Oh, he's not a bad fellow," replied Brandon.

" He's a snob, *pur et simple*—a snob, with the
wardrobe of a tailor's assistant, and the manners
of a valet. You called young Trefalden a snob
just now, and I told you it was a mistake.
Apply the title to this little money-jobber, and I
won't contradict you. The fact is, Brandon, I
abominate him. I wish it was possible to black-
ball him out of the club. If I'd been in town
when he was proposed, I'll be hanged if he should
have ever got in. I can't think what you fellows
were about, to admit him ! "

Charley Burgoyne was a lazy man, and for him
this was a very long and energetic speech. But
the Honourable Edward Brandon only shook his
head in a helpless, irritable way, and repeated his
former assertion.

" I tell you, Burgoyne," he said, " Greatorex
isn't a bad fellow."

Sir Charles Burgoyne shrugged his shoulders, and yawned.

"Oh, very well," he replied. "Have it your own way. I hate argument."

"Castletowers likes him," said the young man. "Castletowers asks him down to Surrey, you see."

"Castletowers is too good-natured by half."

"And Vaughan. . . ."

"Vaughan owes him money, and just endures him."

The Honourable Edward Brandon rubbed his head all over, looking more helpless and more irritable than before. It was a very small head, and there was very little in it.

"Confound him!" groaned he. "He has taken up paper of mine, too. I *must* be civil to him."

Sir Charles Burgoyne gave utterance to a dismal whistle; thrust his hands deep down into his pockets; and said nothing.

"What else can I do?" said Brandon.

"Pay him."

"You might as well tell me to eat him."

"Nonsense. Borrow the money from somebody else."

"I wish I could. I wish I knew whom to ask. I should be so very grateful, you know. It's only two hundred and fifty."

And the young fellow stared hard at the Guardsman, who stared just as hard at the Duke of York's column over the way.

"You can't suggest any one?" he continued, after a moment.

"I, my dear fellow? *Diable!* I haven't an idea."

"You—couldn't manage it for me yourself, I suppose?"

Sir Charles Burgoyne took his hands from his pockets, and his hat from a neighbouring peg.

"Edward Brandon," he said, impressively, "I'm as poor as Saint Simeon Stylites."

"Never heard of the fellow in my life," said Brandon, peevishly. "Who is he?"

"My dear boy, your religious education has been neglected. Look for him in your catechism, and, 'when found, make a note of.'"

"I'll tell you what it is, Burgoyne," said

Brandon, suspicious of " chaff," and, like all weak
people when they are out of temper, slightly
spiteful—" poor, or not poor, you're a clever
fellow at a bargain.   Talk of you're not wanting
a fancy price, indeed!   What's five hundred
guineas if it's not a fancy price, I should like to
know ? "

" *Mon enfant*, you know nothing about it,"
said the Guardsman placidly.

" I know it was an awful lot too much for that
mare and cab."

" The mare and cab were dirt cheap at the
money."

" Cheap! cheap—when to my certain knowledge you only gave a hundred and twenty for
the Lady of Lyons, and have had the best part of
two seasons out of her since ! "

The Beauty listened with an imperturbable
smile, drew on his gloves, buttoned them, adjusted his hat, and, having done all these things
with studied deliberation, replied :—

" My dear Brandon, I really envy your memory.   Cultivate it, my good fellow, and it will
be a credit to you.   *Au revoir*."

With this he went over to the nearest glass, corrected the tie of his cravat, and sauntered towards the door. He had not reached it, however, when he paused, turned, and came back again.

"By-the-by," said he, "if you're in any present difficulty, and actually want that two hundred and fifty . . . *do* you want it?"

"Oh, by Jove, don't I! Never wanted it so much in my life."

"Well, then, there's Trefalden. He's as rich as the Bank of England, and flings his money about like water. Ask him, Brandon. He'll be sure to lend it to you. *Vale.*"

And the baronet once more turned on his heel, leaving his irritable young friend to swear off his indignation as best he could. Whereupon the Honourable Edward Brandon, addressing himself apparently to the Duke of York upon his column, did swear with "bated breath" and remarkable fluency; rubbed his head frantically, till he looked like an electrical doll; and finally betook himself to the billiard-room.

When they were both gone, a gentleman who had been sitting in the adjoining window, entrenched behind, and apparently absorbed in, the "Times" of the day, laid his paper aside; entered a couple of names in his pocket-book, smiling quietly the while; and then left the room. He paused on his way out, to speak to the hall porter.

"I have waited for Mr. Trefalden," he said, "till I can wait no longer. You are sure he has not gone up-stairs?"

"Quite sure, sir."

"Be so good, then, as to give him this card, and say, if you please, that I will call upon him at his chambers to-morrow."

The porter laid the card aside with the new member's letters, of which there were several. It bore the name of William Trefalden.

CHAPTER XVII.

" Mr. Trefalden."

Thus announced by a stately valet, who received him with marked condescension in the ante-chamber, and even deigned to open the door of the reception-room beyond, Mr. Trefalden passed into his cousin's presence. He was not alone. Lord Castletowers and Sir Charles Burgoyne were there; Lord Castletowers leaning familiarly over the back of Saxon's chair, dictating the words of a letter which Saxon was writing; Sir Charles Burgoyne extended at full length on a sofa, smoking a cigarette with his eyes closed. Both visitors were obviously as much at home as if in their own chambers. They had been break-fasting with Saxon, and the table was yet loaded

with pâtés, coffee, liqueurs, and all the luxurious
et cæteras of a second *déjeûner*.

Saxon flung away his pen, sprang forward,
seized his cousin by both hands, and poured forth
a torrent of greetings.

"How good of you to come," he exclaimed,
"after having taken the trouble to go yesterday
to the club! I was so sorry to miss you! I
meant to hunt you up this very afternoon in
Chancery Lane. I have been an ungrateful fellow
not to do so a week ago, and I'm sure I don't
know how to excuse myself. I've thought of you,
Cousin William, every day."

"I should have been sorry to bring you into
the dingy atmosphere of the City," said Mr. Trefalden, pleasantly. "I had far rather see you
thus, enjoying the good things which the gods
have provided for you."

And with this, Mr. Trefalden shook hands with
Lord Castletowers, hoped Lady Castletowers was
well, bowed to Sir Charles Burgoyne, and dropped
into an easy chair.

"You were writing," he said, "when I came
in. Pray go on."

Saxon shook his head.

"Oh, no," he said, shyly, "the letters can wait."

"So can I—and smoke a cigar in the meanwhile."

"They—that is, Lord Castletowers was helping me to write them—telling me what to say, in fact. He calls me 'The Impolite Letter Writer,' and says I must learn to turn fine phrases, and say the elegant things that nobody means."

"The things that nobody means are the things that everybody likes," said the Earl.

"I have often wished," said Burgoyne, from the sofa, "that some clever person would write a handbook of civil speeches—a sort of 'Ready Liar,' you know, or 'Perjuror's Companion.' It would save a fellow so much trouble!"

"I wish there were such a book, if only to teach *you* better manners," retorted Castletowers.

"I don't pretend to have the manners of a lord," said the Beauty, languidly.

"If you were the lord of my manors, you

wouldn't have many to boast of," replied Castletowers, with a light-hearted laugh.

Burgoyne opened his eyes, and took the
cigarette from his mouth.

" Listen to this fellow ! " said he, " this bloated
capitalist, who talks like a Diogenes turned out
of his tub !　Castletowers, I am ashamed of you."

" Compare me to Diogenes, if you like," replied
the Earl; " but to a Diogenes who has a dear old
Elizabethan tub still left, thank Heaven ! and a
few old oaks to shelter it.　Few enough, and old
enough, more's the pity ! "

" And I," said Burgoyne, with a yawn,
" haven't a stick of timber left, barring my genealogical tree.　My last oaks vanished in the last
Derby."

The Earl looked at his watch.

" If this note is to be delivered by two o'clock,"
said he, " it must be finished at once ; and since
Mr. Trefalden gives us leave . . . ."

" I not only give leave," said Mr. Trefalden,
" I entreat."

Saxon took up his pen, and pointing to a heap
of notes on the mantelshelf, said :—

" You will find one there for yourself, Cousin William ; and you must be sure to come."

" Invitations, young man ? "

"Yes, to a dinner at Richmond, next Saturday."

Mr. Trefalden put the note in his pocket unopened ; smoked away with a quiet, meditative smile ; and took a leisurely survey of the room as the dictation proceeded. Not one of its multitudinous details escaped him—not one but told him some anecdote of the last ten days of Saxon's new life. There were several pictures standing about on chairs, or leaning against the walls. Some were painted in oils and some in water colours, and nearly all were views in Switzerland. There were piles of new music ; stacks of costly books in rich bindings ; boxes of cigars and gloves ; a bust of Shakespeare in marble ; a harmonium ; a cabinet of Florentine mosaic-work ; a marvellous Etruscan vase on a pedestal of *verde antico ;* a couple of silver-mounted rifles ; a sideboard loaded with knickknacks in carved ivory, crystal, silver filagree, and egg-shell china ; and a sofa-table heaped with notes, visiting cards, loose silver, and tradesmen's bills. On the chimney-piece stood a pair of bronze tazzas, a silver ink-stand with a little Cupid perched upon the lid, and a *giallo* model of the Parthenon. A gold-headed riding whip, and a pair of foils lay on the top of the harmonium; and a faded bouquet in a tumbler occupied a bracket, from which a French pendule had been ignominiously displaced. William Trefalden was an observant man, and drew his inferences from these trifles. He found out that his young Arcadian was learning to ride, fence, make acquaintances, and spend his money royally. Above all, he took note of the bouquet on the bracket. There was nothing remarkable about it. It was just like five hundred other bouquets that one sees in the course of a season; and yet Mr. Trefalden looked at it more than once, and smiled under cover of a cloud of smoke each time that he did so.

"—*and that you will permit me to have the great pleasure of driving you down in the afternoon*," said Lord Castletowers, dictating over Saxon's shoulder.

"Drive her down!" echoed the scribe, in

dismay. "*I* drive her from London to Richmond?"

"Of course. Why not?"

"I can't. I don't drive well enough. I have never driven anything but an old blind mare in a rickety Swiss charette, in my life. I should break her neck and my own too!"

"Oh, never mind. You can give the reins to Burgoyne, or to me. It doesn't matter."

"Then how shall I put it? Shall I say '*and that you will permit Lord Castletowers to have the pleasure of* . . . .'"

"Nonsense! Write what I told you at first, and leave me to arrange it, when it comes to the point."

Saxon shook his head.

"No, no," said he. "I must not ask to be allowed the pleasure of driving her down, when I know all the time I am not going to do anything of the sort. It wouldn't be true."

A faint blush mounted to the Earl's honest brow; but Sir Charles Burgoyne smiled compassionately.

"Suppose, now," said Saxon, "that I tell her

I've bought a new phaeton, and hope she will accept a seat in it on Saturday—will that do?"

"Famously. She'll of course conclude that you drive, and the rest is easily managed when the time comes. Let's see how it reads . . . . hum . . . . '*which I trust you will honour with your presence; also that you will permit me to offer you a seat in my phaeton, if the day be fine enough for my friends to drive down in open carriages.*'"

"*Open carriages*," repeated Saxon, as his pen travelled to the end of the sentence. "Anything more?"

"No; I think that is enough."

"Then I only add—'*yours very truly, Saxon Trefalden,*' I suppose?"

"Heaven forbid!"

"Isn't it polite enough?" asked Saxon, laughing.

"Polite enough? Didn't I tell you half an hour ago that to be commonly polite is nothing in a case like this? You must approach her on your knees, my dear fellow, and offer up your little Richmond dinner as if it were a burnt sacri-

fice to the immortal gods! Say—'*Condescend,
madam, to accept my respectful homage, and allow
me to subscribe myself, with the profoundest admiration, your obedient and faithful servant, Saxon
Trefalden.*' That's the way to put it, Burgoyne?"

" Oh, unquestionably," yawned that gentleman.
" You can't crowd too much sail."

" May I inquire to which Princess of the Blood
Royal this letter is addressed?" asked Mr. Trefalden.

" To a far greater She than any princess," replied Castletowers. " To the prima donna of the
season—to the Graziana herself!"

Mr. Trefalden slightly elevated his eyebrows
on receiving this tremendous information, but
said nothing.

" And she's the grandest creature!" ejaculated
Saxon, now folding and sealing his note. " Burgoyne introduced me to her last night, behind
the scenes. You can't think what a gracious
manner she has, Cousin William!"

" Really?"

" She gave me that bouquet up there—it had
just been thrown to her."

" How condescending ! "

" Wasn't it ?—and I such an utter stranger—a nobody, you know !   I felt, I assure you, as if I were in the presence of Juno herself.   There, the note's quite ready."

And Saxon, all unconscious of the faint touch of sarcasm in his cousin's voice, lifted up his bright young face with a smile of boyish exultation, and rang the bell.

" Gillingwater, send Curtis at once with this note, and tell him to wait for an answer.   Anybody here ? "

" Young man from Facet and Carat's, sir, with case of jules.   Young man from Cartridge and Trigger's, with harms.   Passle from Colnaggy's ; passle from Breidenback's ; passle from Fortnum and Mason's ; passle from Crammer and Beale's," replied Saxon's magnificent valet.

" The parcels can wait.   The messengers may come in."

Mr. Gillingwater retired, and the " young men " were immediately ushered in ; one with a small mahogany box under his arm ; the other carrying a still smaller morocco case.

The first contained a brace of costly inlaid pistols; the second, three bracelets of different designs.

"By Jove, what pistols!" exclaimed Castle-towers. "Look here, Burgoyne, did you ever see such finish?"

"Never. They might be worn by the sultan."

"They are exact facsimiles of those made for His Highness the Maharajah of Jubblepore," observed the messenger.

Sir Charles examined the weapons with the interest of a connoisseur.

"What a Bashaw you are, Trefalden!" he said. "We shall have you cantering down Rotten-row on a white elephant before long. These are really the most gorgeous pistols I have seen. Who are the bangles for? The Graziana?"

"One of them, if . . . ."

"If what?"

"If you think she would not be offended?"

"Offended, my dear fellow! Is pussy offended if you offer her a cup of milk? or Carlo, if you present him with a bone?"

"What do you mean?" said Saxon, quite shocked at the levity of these comparisons.

"I mean that every woman would sell her soul for a handful of diamonds, and an ounce of wrought gold, and that our fair friend is no exception to the rule. What put it into your head, Trefalden, to give her a bracelet?"

"It was Mr. Greatorex's idea."

"Humph! Just like him. Greatorex has such generous impulses—at other people's expense!"

"I was very much obliged to him for thinking of it," said Saxon, somewhat warmly. "As I am to any friend who is kind enough to tell me what the customs of society are," he added, more gently.

"They are very beautiful bracelets, all three of them," said Lord Castletowers.

"That's right. Which shall I take?"

"The garter set with rubies," said Sir Charles Burgoyne.

"The snake with the diamond head," said the Earl.

"The opals and diamonds," said William Trefalden.

Saxon laughed, and shook his head.

"If you each give me different advice," said he, "what am I to do?"

"Choose for yourself," replied his cousin.

And so Saxon, very diffidently and hesitatingly, chose for himself, and took the one his cousin had preferred.

"And pray what may be the cost of this magnificent trifle?" asked Mr. Trefalden, when the choice was made, and the messengers had made their bows and vanished.

"I have no idea," replied Saxon.

"Do you mean that you have bought it without having made any inquiry as to its price?"

"Of course."

"Pray do you never inquire before you purchase?"

"Never. Why do you smile?"

"Because I fear your tradesmen will charge you at any fabulous rate they please."

"Why, so they could in any case! What do I know, for instance, of opals and diamonds, except that the opal is a hydrate of silica, and that the diamond consists of pure carbon in a crystalline state? They might ask me what price they pleased for this bracelet, and I, in my ignorance of its value, should buy it, just the same."

"It is well for you, Trefalden, that you have the purse of Fortunatus to dip your hand into," said Sir Charles Burgoyne.

"But even Fortunatus must take care that his purse has no hole in the bottom of it," added Mr. Trefalden. "You are a bad financier, my dear Saxon; and you and I must have a little practical conversation some day on these matters. By the way, I have really some business points to discuss with you. When can you give up an hour or two to pure and unmixed boredom?"

"When you please, cousin William."

"Well—this evening?"

"This evening, unfortunately, I have promised to dine at the club with Greatorex, and two or three others, and we are going afterwards to the opera."

"To-morrow evening, then?"

"And to-morrow my new phaeton is coming home, and we are going in it to Blackwall—Lord Castletowers and Sir Charles Burgoyne, I mean."

" Then, on Saturday . . ."

" On Saturday, I hope you will join us at
Richmond. Don't forget it, cousin William. You
have the note, you know, in your pocket."

Mr. Trefalden smiled somewhat gravely.

" Are you already such an Epicurean that you
want the traditional skeleton at your feast ? " said
he. " No, no, Saxon. I am a man of business,
and have no leisure for such symposia. You
must dispense with my grim presence—and I,
apparently, must dispense with yours. I had no
notion that you were such a man of fashion
as to have all your evenings engaged in this
manner."

" I can't think how it is," replied Saxon, in
some confusion. " I certainly have made more
appointments than I was aware of. My friends
are so kind to me, and plan so many things tò
give me pleasure, that—will Sunday do, cousin
William ? You might come up here and dine
with me; or we might . . ."

" I am always engaged on Sundays," said Mr.
Trefalden, drily.

" Then on Monday ? "

"Yes, I can see you on Monday, if you will really be at leisure."

"Of course, I will be at leisure."

"But you must come to me. I shall be very busy, and can only see you after office hours."

"I will come to you, cousin, at any time you please," said Saxon, earnestly.

"At eight in the evening?"

"At eight."

Mr. Trefalden entered the hour and date in his pocket-book, and rose to take his leave.

"I had hoped that you would spare me a day or two next week, Mr. Trefalden," said Lord Castletowers, as they shook hands at parting. "Your cousin has promised to come down, and we have a meet and some parties coming off; and a breath of country air would do you good before the summer sets in."

But Mr. Trefalden shook his head.

"I thank you, Lord Castletowers," he replied; "but it is impossible. I am as firmly chained to Chancery Lane for the next five months as any galley-slave to his oar."

"But, my dear sir, is it worth any man's while

to be a galley-slave, if he can help it?" asked the
Earl.

"Perhaps. It depends on the motive; and
self-imposed chains are never very heavy to the
wearer."

And with this, Mr. Trefalden bowed to both
gentlemen, and left the room, followed by his
cousin.

"That's a quiet, deep fellow," said Burgoyne.

"He is a very gentlemanly, pleasant, clever
man," replied the Earl, "and has been our solicitor for years."

"I don't like him."

"You don't know him."

"True—do you?"

Lord Castletowers hesitated.

"Well, upon my soul," laughed he, "I cannot
say that I do. But, as I tell you, he is my
solicitor, and I like him. I only speak from
my impressions."

"And I from mine. He is not my solicitor,
and I don't like him. He thinks too much, and
says too little."

In the meanwhile, Saxon was warmly wringing

his cousin's hand at the door of the ante-room, and saying, in a low, earnest tone :—

"Indeed you must not suppose I have become a man of fashion, or an Epicurean, cousin William; or that I would not rather—far rather—spend an evening with you than at any of these fine places. I am so very sorry I cannot come to you before Monday."

"Monday will be quite soon enough, my dear Saxon," replied Mr. Trefalden, kindly; "and I am glad to see you so well amused. At eight o'clock, then?"

"Yes, at eight. You will see how punctual I shall be. And you must give me some good advice, cousin William, and always tell me of my faults—won't you?"

"Humph! That will depend on circumstances, and yourself. In the meanwhile, don't buy any more diamond bracelets without first inquiring the price."

CHAPTER XVIII.

TIMON.

"It is good to be merry and wise," saith an old song; but every man cannot be a laughing philosopher, and though it is comparatively easy to be either merry or wise "upon occasion," it is supremely difficult to be both at the same time. The two conditions mix almost as reluctantly as oil and water, and youth seldom makes even an effort to combine them. Happy youth, whose best wisdom it is, after all, to be merry while it may! Which of us would not gladly barter this bitter wisdom of later years for but a single season—nay, a single day—of that happy thoughtless time when the simplest jest provoked a laugh, and the commonest wayside flower had a beauty long since faded, and all life was a pleasant carnival? What would we not give to

believe once more in the eternity of college friend-
ships, and the immortality of prize poems?—to
feel our hearts beat high over the pages of
Plutarch and Livy?—to weep delicious tears for
the woes of Mrs. Haller, and to devour the old
romances with the old omnivorous relish?

Alas! the college friend and the prize poem
are alike forgotten; Sir George Cornewall Lewis
has laid his ruthless hand upon our favourite
heroes; our souls abhor the very name of Kotze-
bue; and we could no more revive our interest
in those two mounted cavaliers who might have
been seen spurring by twilight across a lonely
heath in the west of England some two hundred
and odd years ago, than we could undertake to
enjoy the thirteen thousand pages of Mademoiselle Scudéry's Grand Cyrus. Aye, that pleasant
dream is indeed over; but its joys are "lodg'd
beyond the reach of fate," and of the remem-
brance of them no man can disinherit us. Have
we not all lived in Arcadia?

Wisdom apart, however, what more commend-
able merriment may there be than a dinner at
Richmond when the year and the guests are

young, and the broad landscape lies steeped in
sunshine, and the afternoon air is sweet with
new-mown hay, and the laugh follows the jest
as quickly and gaily as the frothing champagne
follows the popping of the corks? Now and
then a tiny skiff with one white sail skims down
the molten gold of the broad river. The plumy
islands and the wooded flats look hazy in the
tender mist of sunset. A pleasant sound of gay
voices and chinking glasses finds its way now
and then from the open window below, or the
adjoining balcony; and, perhaps, the music of a
brass band comes to us from the lower town,
harmonised by distance.

Thus bright and propitious was it on the
eventful day of Saxon's " little dinner; " and
care had been taken by his. friends that every
detail of the entertainment should be as faultless
as the weather itself. The guests had all been
driven down in open carriages; the costliest
dinner that money could ensure, or taste devise,
was placed before them; and the best room in
the famous hotel was pre-engaged for the occasion. It had seldom held a more joyous party.

Lord Castletowers and Major Vaughan were there of course, having run up from Surrey for the day; Sir Charles Burgoyne, serenely insolent; the Hon. Edward Brandon, with his hair standing up like the wig of an electrified doll, from inward excitement and outward rubbing; Mr. Lawrence Greatorex, looking, perhaps, somewhat abstracted from time to time, but talking fluently; two other Erectheum men, both very young and prone to laughter, and both highly creditable to their tailors and bootmakers; and last, though not least, the Graziana and her party. For actresses, like misfortunes, never come alone. Like Scottish chieftains, they travel with a "tail," and have an embarrassing aptitude for bringing their uninvited "tail" on all kinds of inconvenient occasions. In the present instance, the heroine of the day had contented herself with only two sisters and a brother; and her young host not only welcomed them with all his honest heart, but thought it very kind and condescending on her part to bring them at all. The brother was a gloomy youth, who said little, ate a great deal, and watched the company in a

furtive manner over the rim of his wine-glass.
The sisters were fat, black-eyed little souls, who
chattered, flirted, and drank champagne inces-
santly. As for the prima donna herself, she was
a fine, buxom, laughter-loving creature of about
twenty years of age, as little like a Juno, and as
much like a grown-up child as it is only possible
for a Neapolitan woman to be. She could be
majestic enough upon the stage, or in the green-
room; but she never carried her dignity beyond
the precincts of the opera house. She put it on
with her rouge, and left it in her dressing-room
with the rest of her theatrical wardrobe, when the
evening's work was over. She laughed at everything that was said, whether she understood it
or not; and she was delighted with everything
—with the drive, with the horses, with the mail
phaeton, with the weather, with the dinner, with
the guests, and with her host; and when the
ice was brought to table—a magnificent, many-
coloured triumph of art—she clapped her hands,
like a child at sight of a twelfthcake.

"Now's the time for the bracelet, Saxon,"
whispered Lord Castletowers, when the wreck

of this triumph was removed, and the sidecloths were rolled away for dessert.

Saxon looked aghast.

" What shall I say ?" said he.

" Oh, I don't know—something graceful, and not too long."

" But I can't.   I haven't an idea."

" Never mind; she wouldn't understand it if you had.   Say anything."

" Can't you say it for me ? "

" Impossible, my dear fellow !   You might as well ask me to kiss her for you."

Which was such a tremendous supposition, that Saxon blushed scarlet, and had not a word to say in reply.

" Ah, *traditor !*   Why do you speak secrets ?" said the prima donna, with a pout.

" Because he is a conspirator, signora," replied the Earl.

" A conspirator?   *Cielo !*"

" It is quite true," said Burgoyne, promptly. " There's a deadly mine of cracker bonbons in the room below, and Trefalden's presently going to say something so sparkling that it will fire the train, and we shall all be blown into the middle of the next century."

The prima donna sang a roulade expressive of terror.

"But the worst is yet to come. This plot, signora, is entirely against yourself," said Castletowers. Then, dropping his voice, "out with it, man," he added. "You couldn't have a better opening."

So Saxon pulled the morocco case out of his pocket, and presented it with as much confusion and incoherence as if it had been a warrant.

The signora screamed with rapture, invoked her brother and sisters, flew to the window with her treasure, flashed it to and fro in every possible light, and for the first five minutes could talk nothing but her native patois.

"But, signore, you must be a great prince!" she exclaimed, when at length she returned to her place at the dinner-table.

"Indeed, I am nothing of the sort," replied Saxon, laughing.

"*E bellissimo, questo braccioletto!* But why do you give him to me?"

"From no other reason than my desire to please you, bella donna," replied Saxon. "The Greeks believed that the opal had power to confer popularity on its wearer; but I do not offer you these opals with any such motive. Your talisman is your voice."

"Bravo, Trefalden!" laughed the Earl. "That was very well said. *Comme l'esprit vient aux fils!*"

"A neat thing spoilt," muttered Greatorex to his next neighbour. "He should have praised her eyes. She knows all about her voice."

"And do you suppose she doesn't know all about her eyes, too?" asked his neighbour, who chanced to be Major Vaughan.

"No doubt; but then a woman is never tired of being admired for her beauty. The smallest pastille of praise is as acceptable to her, in its way, as a holocaust of incense. But as to her voice, *c'est autre chose.* What is one compliment more or less after the nightly applauses of the finest audience in Europe?"

In the meanwhile, the two Erectheum young men, oppressed apparently by the consciousness of how much they owed to their boots and waist-coats, took refuge in each other's society, and talked about a horse. Neither of them kept a horse, or hoped to keep a horse; and yet the subject seemed bound up, in some occult way, with the inner consciousness of both. They discussed this mysterious animal in solemn whispers, all the way down from London to Richmond; alluded to him despondingly during dinner; and exchanged bets upon him in a moody and portentous manner at dessert. Apart from this overwhelming topic, they were light-hearted young fellows enough; but the horse was their Nemesis, and rode them down continually.

As for the "tail," it went to work as vigorously upon the dessert as upon the twelve preceding courses. The plump sisters evidently looked upon Moet as pure Pierian, and had taken Pope's advice to heart; while the gloomy brother, inaccessible as fort Gibraltar, seemed only intent on provisioning himself against a long blockade. But even the best of dinners must end, and coffee came at last. Then one of the Erectheum young men, emboldened by sparkling drinks,

asked the prima donna for a song.   She laughed
and shook her head; but the assembled company
looked aghast.

"I cannot," said she.   "My voice is a bird in
one little cage, and my *Impressario* guards the
key."

Sir Charles Burgoyne darted a dreadful glance
at the offender.

"My dear lady," he said, "pray do not say a
word.   We all know, or ought to know, that
your operatic contract forbids anything of the
kind; and even if it were not so, we should not
presume to ask so great a favour.   It is entirely
a mistake—a great mistake—on the part of this
young gentleman."

"I—I am very sorry," stammered the unlucky
neophyte.

"And I am sorry," said the songstress, good-
naturedly.   "I should sing for you if I dared."

"Thou must not think of it, *sorellina*," interposed her brother, in his rapid Neapolitan.
"Remember the penalty."

"The Signora Graziana must do nothing to
offend the manager," said Lord Castletowers,

who was familiar with every dialect of the Italian.

"Certainly not," exclaimed Saxon. "Not for the world."

Then, turning to Burgoyne, he whispered— "What is it all about? Why should he be offended because she sang for us?"

"He would have me pay him one hundred pounds," said the prima donna, whose ears were quick.

"A hundred pounds fine, you know," explained Burgoyne. "'Tis in his bond, and the man's a very Shylock with his ducats."

Saxon laughed aloud.

"Is that all?" said he. "Oh, never mind, *bella donna*—I'll pay him his hundred pounds, and welcome."

And so a piano was brought in from another room, and the Graziana sang to them divinely, not one song, but a dozen.

"Perhaps our friend the *Impressario* may not hear of it, after all," said Mr. Greatorex, when the music was over, and they were preparing to return to town.

"Let us all take a solemn oath of secresy,"
suggested Sir Charles Burgoyne.

But Saxon would not hear of it.

"No, no," said he. "The fine has been fairly
forfeited, and shall be fairly paid. Let no
man's soul be burthened with a secret on my
account. I will send Shylock his cheque to-morrow morning. Ladies, the carriages are at the
door."

"I had heard that our Amphitryon did not
know the value of money," said Mr. Greatorex,
as they went down-stairs, "and now I believe it.
Why, this little affair, my lord, take it from first
to last, must have been set to the tune of something like five hundred pounds!"

"Well, I suppose it has," replied Castletowers,
"including the bracelet."

"A modern Timon—eh?"

"Nay, I hope not. A modern Mæcenas, if
you like. It is a name of better augury."

"I fear he dispenses his gold more after the
fashion of Timon than of Mæcenas," replied the
banker, drily.

"He is a splendid fellow," said the Earl, with

enthusiasm; "and his lavish generosity is by no means the noblest part of his character."

"But he behaved like a fool about that hundred pounds. Of course, we should all have kept the secret, and . . . ."

"I beg your pardon, Mr. Greatorex," interrupted the Earl, somewhat stiffly. "In my opinion, Mr. Trefalden simply behaved like a man of honour."

CHAPTER XIX.

MR. TREFALDEN ON THE DOMESTIC MANNERS AND CUSTOMS OF LAWYERS IN GENERAL.

"So, my young cousin, you have not yet lost all your primitive virtues," said Mr. Trefalden, as Saxon, heralded by Mr. Keckwitch, made his appearance on the threshold of the lawyer's private room at eight o'clock precisely on Monday evening.

"I hope I have parted from none that I ever possessed," replied Saxon; "but to what particular virtue do you allude?"

"To your punctuality, young man. You are as true to time as on that memorable morning when we breakfasted together at Reichenau, and you tasted Lafitte for the first time. You have become tolerably familiar with the flavour, since then."

"Indeed I have," replied Saxon, with a smile and a sigh.

"And with a good many other flavours as well, I imagine. Why, let me see, that was on the seventh of March, and here is the beginning of the third week in April—scarcely five weeks ago, Saxon!"

"It seems like five centuries."

"I dare say it does. You have crowded a vast number of impressions into a very short space of time. But then you are rich in the happy adaptability of youth and can bear the shock of revolution."

"I try to bear it as well I can," replied Saxon, laughingly. "It isn't very difficult."

"No—the lessons of pleasure and power are soon learnt; and, by the way, the art of dress also. You are quite a swell, Saxon."

The young fellow's face crimsoned.

He could not get over that awkward habit of blushing, do what he would.

"I hope not," he said. "I am what fate and my tailor have made me. Castletowers took me to his own man, and he has done as he liked with me."

"So that, to paraphrase the kingly state, your virtues are your own, and your shortcomings are your tailor's? Nay, don't look uncomfortable. You are well dressed; but not too well dressed —which, to my thinking, is precisely as a gentleman should be."

"I don't wish to be a 'swell,'" said Saxon.

"Nor are you one. And now tell me something about yourself. How do you like this new life?"

"It bewilders me," said Saxon. "It dazzles me. It takes my breath away. I feel as if London were a huge circus, all dust, and roar, and glitter, and I being carried round it, in a great chariot race. It frightens me sometimes, —and yet I enjoy it. There is so much to enjoy!"

"But you thought it a 'dreary' place at first," said Mr. Trefalden, with his quiet smile.

"Because I was a stranger, and knew no one —because the very roar and flow of life along the streets only made my solitude the heavier. But that's all changed now, thanks to you."

"Thanks to me, Saxon?"

"Of course. Don't I owe that dear 'fellow Castletowers' acquaintance to you? And if I hadn't known him, how should I have got into the Erectheum? How should I have known Burgoyne, and Greatorex, and Brandon, and Fitz-Hugh, and Dalton, and all the other fellows? And they are so kind to me—it's perfectly incredible how kind they are, and what trouble they take to oblige and please me!"

"Indeed?" said the lawyer, drily.

"Yes, that they do; and I should be worse than ungrateful if I did not like a place where I have so many friends. Then, again, I have so much to do—so much to think of—so much to learn. Why, it would take half a life-time only to see all the picture galleries in London, and study the Etruscan vases in the British Museum!"

Mr. Trefalden could not help laughing.

"You droll boy!" said he. "Do you mean to tell me that you divide your attentions between pretty prima donnas and cinerary urns?"

"I mean that I was in the Etruscan room for three hours this morning, and that we have a tazza at Rotzberg of a kind of which you have not a single specimen in the collection—red, with red *bassi rilievi*. What do you say to that?"

"That I would not give five farthings for all the old pottery in Europe."

"Yes, you would, if you once learned to look upon it as history. Now the pottery of Etruria . . ."

"My dear Saxon," interposed Mr. Trefalden, "as you are great, be merciful. Spare me the pottery of Etruria, and tell me a little more about yourself. You are learning to ride, are you not?"

"Yes, I can ride pretty well already; and I have a fencing lesson every other morning, and I am learning to drive. But I don't get on quite so well with the whip as with the foils. I have an awkward habit of locking my wheels with other people's, and getting to the wrong side of the road."

"Awkward habits, indeed," said Mr. Trefalden; "especially in Rotten Row."

"And—and I am learning to dance, also," said Saxon, with a shy laugh.

"In short, what with finishing your education, giving suburban dinners, and cultivating the fine arts, your time is tolerably well occupied."

"It is, indeed. I never seem to have a moment to spare."

"Humph! And pray may I ask how much money you have spent during these last three weeks?"

"I haven't the least idea."

"I suspected as much. Kept no accounts, I suppose?"

"None whatever."

Mr. Trefalden smiled significantly, but said nothing.

"I suppose it's very wrong," said Saxon. "I suppose I ought to have put it all down in a book?"

"Undoubtedly."

"But then I know nothing of book-keeping; indeed, I scarcely yet know the real value of money. But if you will tell me what I ought to do, I will try. Gillingwater, can help me, too. *He* knows."

"Gillingwater is your valet, is he not? Where did you hear of him?"

"Greatorex recommended him to me. He is a most invaluable fellow. I don't know what I should do without him."

"And you have a groom, I suppose?"

"I have two grooms."

"Two? My dear boy, what can you want with more than one?"

"I don't know. Burgoyne said I couldn't do with less—but then, you know, I keep five horses."

"Indeed?"

"Yes; one for the cab, two for riding, and two for the mail phaeton."

"And you keep them at livery, of course?"

"Yes; Burgoyne said it was the best way; and that the beasts were sure to be ill-fed if I hired stabling and left it to the men. He knows so much about horses."

"Evidently. It was he who sold you that mare and cab, was it not?"

"To be sure it was; and then I have bought all the rest under his advice. I assure you, cousin William, I don't believe any fellow ever had such friends!"

Mr. Trefalden coughed, and looked at his watch.

"Well," he said, "we must not forget that I have brought you down here to-night, Saxon, for a serious conference. Shall we have some coffee first, to filter the dust from our brains?"

Whereupon, Saxon assenting, the lawyer rang the bell and coffee was brought. In the meanwhile, the young man had made the tour of the room, inspected the law books on the shelves, examined the door of the safe, peeped out of the window, and ascertained the date of the map hanging over the fireplace. This done, he resumed his chair, and said, with more frankness than politeness :—

"I'd as soon live in a family vault as in this dismal place! Is it possible, cousin William, that you have no other home?"

"The greater part of my life is passed here," replied Mr. Trefalden, sipping his coffee. "I admit that the decorations are not in the highest style of art; but they answer the purpose well enough."

"And you actually live here, day and night, summer and winter?"

"Why no—not altogether. I have a den—a mere den—a few miles from town, in which I hide myself at night, like a beast of prey."

"It is a relief to my mind to know that," said Saxon. "I should like to see your den. Why didn't you let me come to you there to-night?"

"Because you are not fat enough."

"Not fat enough?" repeated Saxon, laughing.

"I admit no man, unless to devour him. Lawyers are ogres, my dear fellow—and that den of mine is paved with the bones of slaughtered clients."

Saying which, Mr. Trefalden put an end to the subject by ringing the bell, and sending for Mr. Keckwitch.

"You may close the office and go, Keckwitch," said he. "I do not want you any more this evening."

Mr. Keckwitch looked at his employer with eyes that had no more speculation in them than if they had been boiled.

"I beg your pardon, sir," he replied with husky

placidity, " but perhaps you forget Rogers's case. I am bound to go through the papers to-night."

" Then you can take them home with you. I have private business with this gentleman, and wish to be alone—you understand? Alone."

A pale light flashed into Mr. Keckwitch's eyes —flashed and vanished. But it did not impart an agreeable expression to his countenance.

" And when you have put all straight, and turned off the gas, please to let me know, that I may lock the office door on the inside."

The head clerk retired without a word, followed by the keen eye of his employer.

" If I were to become a rich man to-morrow," said he, with a bitter smile, " the first elegant superfluity in which I should indulge, would be the kicking of that fellow all the way along Chancery Lane. It is a luxury that would be cheap at any price the Court might award."

" If you have so bad an opinion of him, why do you keep him ? " asked Saxon.

" For the reason that one often keeps an aching tooth. He is a useful grinder, and helps me to polish off the bones that I was telling you about just now."

Mr. Trefalden then saw his head clerk off the premises, locked the outer door, made up the fire, put the shade on the lamp (he always liked, he said, to spare his eyes), and drew his chair to the table.

CHAPTER XX.

MR. KECKWITCH banished, and the coffee-cups pushed aside, William Trefalden uttered a little preliminary cough, and said,

"Now, Saxon, to business."

Saxon was all attention.

"In the first place," he began, "you have a large fortune in money; and it is highly important that so weighty a sum should be advantageously placed. By advantageously placed, I mean laid out in the purchase of land, lent on mortgage, or otherwise employed in such a manner as to bring you large returns. And I assure you I have not ceased, since your affairs have been in my hands, to make inquiry in every quarter where inquiry was likely to lead to anything useful."

"I'm sure it's very kind of you," murmured Saxon, vaguely.

"The great difficulty," continued Mr. Trefalden, "is the largeness of the sum. It is comparatively easy to dispose of fifty, or a hundred, or even of five hundred thousand pounds; but nobody either wants to borrow, or could give security, for such a sum as four millions. Not that I should wish to see your all placed upon a single venture. Far from it. I would not advise such a step, though the Russian government were the borrower. But neither do I wish to spread your property over too large a surface. It is a course attended with great inconvenience and great expense. Do you quite follow me?"

"Not in the least," said Saxon, to whom the language of the money market was about as intelligible as a cuneiform inscription.

"Well, you understand that your money ought to be invested?"

"I thought it was invested. It's in Drummond's bank."

"Not so. The bulk of your fortune consists

of Government stock; but a very considerable
sum which I had expected to invest for you before
now, and which, if you remember, we sold out of
the funds when you first came to London, is
temporarily deposited at Drummond's, where at
present it brings you no interest. My object,
however, is to do with this what I hope to do in
time with the whole of your money—namely,
invest it safely at a high rate of interest. By
these means you will enjoy an ample income, but
leave your capital untouched."

"Shall I, indeed?" said Saxon, struggling to
conceal a yawn. "That is very curious."

"Not curious at all, if one but understands the
first principles of banking. Have you no idea of
what interest is?"

"Oh dear yes," replied Saxon, briskly, "I
know all about that. Greatorex explained it to
me. Interest means two and a half per cent."

Mr. Trefalden shifted the position of his chair,
and turned the lamp in such a manner that the
light fell more fully on Saxon's face, and left his
own in shadow.

"Two and a half per cent!" he repeated.

"That was a very limited statement on the part of Mr. Greatorex. Interest may mean anything, from one per cent. up to a hundred, or a hundred thousand. He cannot have offered that assertion as an explanation of general facts. Do you remember the conversation that led to it?"

"Not clearly; but he was talking very much as you have just been talking, and he said they would give me two and a half per cent. at their bank, if I liked to put my money in it."

"Humph! and your reply?"

"I said you managed everything of that sort for me, and that I would ask you to see to it."

"Meaning that you would ask me to transfer your money from Drummond's to Greatorex's?"

"If you please."

"Then I certainly do not please; and as long as you continue to attach the slightest value to my opinion, you will not place a penny in their hands."

Saxon looked aghast.

"Oh, but—but I promised," said he.

"Precisely what I expected to hear you say. I felt sure you had been trapped into a promise of some kind."

"I can't break my word," said Saxon, reso-
lutely.

Mr. Trefalden shrugged his shoulders.

"I can't let you ruin yourself," he replied.
"Greatorex and Greatorex are on the verge of
bankruptcy; and I have private information which
leads me to believe they must stop payment before
the week is out."

The young man stared at him in silence. He
neither knew what to say, nor what to think.

"And now," said his cousin, "tell me all that
took place, as nearly as you can remember it.
First of all, I suppose, Mr. Laurence Greatorex
kindly volunteered to explain to you the system
under which money can be made to produce
interest; and, having shown you how it was part
of the business of a banker to pay interest on
deposits, he proposed to take your money, and
allow you two and a half per cent?"

Saxon nodded.

"You referred the proposition to me, and Mr.
Greatorex was not best pleased to find that you
relied so much upon my judgment."

"How do you know that?" exclaimed Saxon.

" He then enlarged on the dangers of high interest, and the troublesome nature of investments in·land; pointed out the advantages of the deposit system; and ended by extracting your promise for . . . how much?"

"Who *can* have told you all this?"

"Tell me first whether I am correct?"

"Word for word."

Mr. Trefalden leaned back in his chair and laughed—a little soft, satisfied laugh, like an audible smile.

"I have a familiar demon, Saxon," said he. "His name is Experience; and he tells me a great many more things than are dreamt of in your philosophy. But you have not yet answered my first question—how much?"

"He said it was a very bad plan to lock up one's money—'lock up' was the phrase, I am sure —and that I should find it so convenient to be able to draw mine out whenever I chose. And then . . . ."

"And then you agreed with him, of course. Go on."

"And then he said he supposed I would not

mind going to the extent of five hundred thousand with their house, and . . . ."

"Five hundred thousand! Had he the incredible impudence to ask you for five hundred thousand?"

"Indeed, Cousin William, it seemed to me, from the way in which he put it, that Mr. Greatorex had only my interest in view."

"How probable!"

"He said that it could make no difference to them; and that one person's thousands were no more to them, in the way of business, than another's."

"And you believed him?"

"Of course I believed him."

"And promised him the five hundred thousand?"

"Yes."

"Then it's a promise that will have to be broken, young man, that is all. Nay, don't look so unhappy. I will take all the burden from your shoulders. A lawyer can do these things easily enough, and offend no one. Besides, no man is bound to fling his money away with his eyes open. If you were to pay in that five hun-

dred thousand pounds to-morrow morning, it would
all be in the pockets of Sir Samuel's creditors
before night.   It would help the firm to stave off
the evil day, and you would most likely get your
two and a half per cent.; but I *know* that you
would never see one farthing of the principal
again—and Laurence Greatorex knows that I
know it."

"But—but I have not told you quite all yet,"
stammered Saxon, whose face had been getting
graver and graver with every word that Mr.
Trefalden uttered.   "I have given him a cheque
for half."

It was well for Mr. Trefalden that the shade
fell on him where he sat, and concealed the storm
that swept across his features at this announce-
ment.   It came and went like a swift shadow;
but, practised master of himself as he was, he
could no more have controlled the expression of
his face at that moment than he could have controlled a thunder-cloud up in the heavens.

"You have given Mr. Greatorex a cheque for
two hundred and fifty thousand pounds?" he
said, after a momentary pause.

" I know it was very wrong—I know I ought to have consulted you first ! " exclaimed Saxon, quite overwhelmed by the magnitude of his error.

" Never mind that at present," replied the lawyer, coldly. " The mischief is done, and we have only to try if any of the money is recoverable. When did you give it to him ? "

" Just now—after dinner."

" To-day ?   After three o'clock ? "

" Not an hour ago. We met at the club; he asked me to dine with him . . . ."

" And when you told him you were to see me this evening, he got you to sign the cheque out of hand ! " interposed Mr. Trefalden, eagerly. " Clever—very clever ; but not quite clever enough, for all that ! "

Saying which, the lawyer seized paper and pen, and began writing rapidly. Having scribbled three or four lines, he pushed them across the table, and said :—

" Read that, and sign it."

It was an order upon the Drummond's firm to refuse payment of all cheques signed by Mr. Saxon Trefalden, until further notice.

"But suppose," said Saxon, "that he has cashed it already?"

"He can't cash it, you foolish boy, till the bank opens to-morrow morning; and by that time it will be too late. I shall instantly take a cab, and go down with this paper to the private house of the chief cashier; and, to make assurance doubly sure, Keckwitch shall be at the bank to-morrow morning when the doors open. Lucky for you, my fine fellow, that you committed this little folly after three o'clock in the day!"

Saxon signed the paper somewhat reluctantly, and Mr. Trefalden put it into his pocket-book.

"Our business conference must wait," said he, "till this affair is settled. Shall you be at home and alone to-morrow at twelve, if I come up for an hour's talk?"

"I will be at home and alone, of course," replied Saxon; "but I am going down into Surrey by the three-o'clock express."

"To Castletowers?"

"Yes—for a week or ten days."

Mr. Trefalden hesitated.

"What I have to say to you must be said quietly and thoroughly," observed he, musingly. "And if you are very stupid indeed, and want a great deal of explanation . . . ."

"Which is quite certain!" interrupted Saxon, laughing.

"Which I am afraid is quite certain—an hour will not be enough."

"Will you come at eleven?"

Mr. Trefalden took up a manuscript book, and examined one or two consecutive pages before replying.

"I will not come at all," he said, closing it decisively, and taking up his hat. "I will run down to you at Castletowers instead, on Thursday morning. The entries in my engagement-book show nothing of great importance for that day, and I know the Earl will be pleased to receive me. I believe I can even manage to dine there, and return by the last train at ten."

"That *is* good!" exclaimed Saxon, heartily; "and a day out of town will invigorate you for a month."

So it was settled; and Mr. Trefalden turned

off the last of the gas, and let his cousin out in
the dark.

"I will send you a line in the morning just to
say that all's well at Drummond's," said the
lawyer, as they shook hands in the street below;
"but you must give me your word of honour
to sign no more cheques till after Wednesday;
and, above all, never again to transact any
important business without first taking my
advice."

"Indeed, Cousin William, I never will," replied Saxon, penitently.

"And if your disinterested friend comes to
you in his wrath to-morrow morning, refer him
to me. My nerves are strong, and I can bear any
amount of vituperation."

"I suppose he will be very much annoyed,"
said Saxon.

"Annoyed? He will go raging up and down,
seeking whom he may devour. But what does
that matter? His anger will not fall upon you,
but upon your legal adviser. And I am not
afraid that he will eat me. Lawyers are indi-
gestible."

Whereupon they again shook hands, and went their separate ways; Mr. Trefalden's way being to Bayswater, where dwelt the chief cashier in the bosom of his family, and Saxon's to his stall at the opera.

CHAPTER XXI.

"Mr. Greatorex wishes to know, sir, if you can give him five minutes' private conversation."

It was not quite a quarter past ten, and Saxon, who had taken a riding lesson before breakfast, was loitering over a book, with the breakfast service still upon the table. He laid the volume hastily down, and desired that Mr. Greatorex might be shown in. He was no moral coward; but he felt decidedly uncomfortable when he heard the quick ring of the banker's high-heeled boots on the polished floor of the antechamber.

Mr. Greatorex came in, shut the door in Gillingwater's face, flung a crumpled slip of paper on the table, and said in a voice that quivered with suppressed passion :—

"You have thought fit, Mr. Trefalden, to stop

the payment of this cheque.   May I inquire with what motive?"

He kept his hat on, and the face beneath it was at a white heat, even to the lips.

"I am really very sorry, Greatorex," said Saxon, nervously; "but I ought never to have given it to you. My cousin manages all my affairs, and I had no business to interfere with his arrangements. He objects to your offer, and —and I am obliged to decline it. But why won't you shake hands with me?"

Mr. Greatorex put his hands behind his back.

"You have insulted me," he said, "and . . . ."

"Not intentionally!" interrupted Saxon. "Upon my honour, not intentionally."

The banker heard him with a bitter smile.

"Pshaw!" he said, scornfully. "We all know what intentions are worth. Yours were certainly not very friendly when you exposed me just now to the grins and sneers of every petty clerk in Drummond's office. Pray did it not occur to you that the position might be the reverse of agreeable; or that it might affect my credit some- what unpleasantly among my brother bankers?"

"I feared, indeed, that I might be so unfortunate as to inconvenience you, Mr. Greatorex,"
replied Saxon, with dignity; "and I tell you
again that I am sorry for it. But I had no
thought of insulting you."

"Inconvenience!" echoed Greatorex, fiercely.
"Good God, man, you have ruined me!"

"Ruined you?"

"Ay, ruined me—me and mine—my father,
who is an old man of sixty-eight—my sisters,
who are both unmarried. Curse you! how do
you like that?"

And with this he flung himself into a chair,
and sat drumming on the table with his clenched
hands.

Saxon was inexpressibly shocked.

"You must explain this to me," he faltered.
"I do not understand—indeed I do not!"

Greatorex glared up at him vindictively, but
made no reply.

"I would not willingly injure my worst enemy,
if I had one," continued the young fellow, with
tears in his voice, if not in his eyes; "much less
one whom I have eaten and drunk with, and

looked upon as my friend. What do you mean
when you say that I have ruined you?"

"Simply that we shall be in the Gazette
to-morrow. You understand that, I suppose?"

The coarse nature of the man had all come to
the surface under this powerful test, and he took
no pains to hide it. He was literally drunk with
rage. Saxon, however, saw his condition, and,
ignorant as he was of human nature, by some
fine instinct, understood and pitied it.

"But why need the withdrawal of this sum
work you so much evil?" he said, gently. "You
are surely no worse off without it to-day than you
were yesterday."

"This is why—since you *will* have it! We
wanted money—money and time—for we have
met with some ugly losses that we didn't choose
to tell the world about; and we knew we could
pull through, if we had the chance."

"Well?"

"Well, there are three or four firms that
have heavy claims upon us, and are getting
troublesome. Relying on your cheque, I

wrote to them last night, and desired them to draw upon us any time after one o'clock to-day. They will draw—and the bank will stop payment."

Saxon sprang to his feet, and seized the cheque, which was still lying where the banker had thrown it.

"No, no," he cried, "not through my act, Greatorex—Heaven forbid! How much do you want, to meet these claims to-day?"

"There's one of twenty-two thousand, six hundred and forty-five pounds," said the other, still sullenly, but in an altered tone. "That's the heaviest. Another of eighteen thousand, two hundred and three fifteen; one of ten thousand; and one of seven thousand, nine hundred and eleven. Fifty-eight thousand, seven hundred and fifty-nine pounds fifteen shillings, in all."

Saxon flew to the bell, and rang it furiously.

"A Hansom from the stand, Gillingwater," said he, "and choose the best horse among them." Then, snatching up his hat—"Greatorex," he added, "I would drive you to Drum-

mond's this instant, if I could; but I won't break
my word.   I gave William my solemn promise
last night to do nothing without consulting him,
and I must go down to Chancery Lane first.   But
you shall have the money long enough before one
—nay, don't shake your head.   It still wants
twenty minutes to eleven, and I'll be back in
three-quarters of an hour ! "

"Pooh ! " said the banker, impatiently.   " I
dare say you mean it; but he won't let you do it.
I know him."

Saxon's eyes flashed.

"Then you don't know *me*," said he.   "The
money is my own, and I swear you shall have it.
How much do you say it is ? "

" Fifty-eight thousand, seven hundred and . .."

"Then fifty-nine thousand will do, and that's
easier to remember.   Come, old fellow, jump into
my cab with me.   I can take you as far as
Chancery Lane, and you'll see me back in Lombard Street before one o'clock."

CHAPTER XXII.

TELEMACHUS SHOWS THAT HE HAS A WILL OF
HIS OWN.

UNLIKE the great ocean which, however racked by hurricane and storm, sleeps in eternal calm but a little way beneath the tossing waves, Mr. Trefalden kept all his tempests down below, and presented to the world a surface of unvarying equanimity. No man ever knew what went on under that "glassy cool" exterior. Cyclones might rage in the far depths of his nature, and those who were looking in his face saw no ripple, heard no echo, of the strife within. It was just thus when Saxon burst in upon him at about eleven o'clock that Tuesday morning, brimful of compassion for the perplexities of the house of Greatorex, and burning to relieve them at the moderate cost of fifty-nine thousand pounds sterling.

Mr. Trefalden was furious; but he smiled, nevertheless, and heard Saxon quite patiently from beginning to end of his story.

" But this is pure nonsense and Quixotism," said he, when the young man came to a pause for want of breath. "What's Greatorex to you, or you to Greatorex? Why should you recklessly sacrifice a sum which is in itself a handsome fortune, to oblige a man who has no claim whatever on your sympathies, or your purse ? "

" I can't let him be ruined ! " cried Saxon, impetuously.

" Why not? He would not have hesitated to ruin you. He would have swept your whole property into his rotten bank, and have allowed you one per cent. less than the current rate of interest."

" I can't tell how that may be," said Saxon; "but I gave him my cheque, and he acted on the faith of it. I must not let him suffer."

" But he would have suffered, sooner or later. Did I not tell you last night that the Greatorexes were on the verge of bankruptcy, and that I

believed they must stop payment before the week
was out?   Don't you remember that?"

"Yes—I remember it."

"Then you must surely see that your cheque
can be in no sense the cause of their ruin?   At
the worst, it but hastens the event by a few days."

"I see that I have no right, and, Heaven
knows! no wish to hasten it by a single hour."

"But, my dear Saxon   .   .   ."

"But, my dear cousin William, Laurence
Greatorex has an old father and two sisters, and
he and I have been on terms of good fellowship
together for this month past, and I'm determined
to stand by him."

"Oh, if you are determined, Saxon, that puts
an end to the matter," said Mr. Trefalden, coldly.
"But in this case, why consult me at all?"

"I didn't come to consult you, cousin; but I
had given you my word not to sign away any
more money till after Thursday, and I felt bound
to let you know what I was about to do."

Mr. Trefalden looked very grave.

"I confess that I am disappointed," he said.
"I had hoped to find my opinion more valued by

you, Saxon. I had also hoped that you would look upon me as something more than your lawyer—as your friend, adviser, guide."

"Why, so I do!" cried the young man, eagerly.

"Pardon me; I do not think so."

"Then you do me injustice; for I put a priceless value on your opinion and your friendship."

"Your present wilfulness disproves your words, Saxon," said his cousin.

"I know it does; but then I also know that I am acting upon impulse, and not according to the laws of worldly wisdom. I have no doubt that you are perfectly right, and that I am utterly wrong—but still I cannot be happy if I do not, for once, indulge my folly."

Seeing that it was useless to push the argument further, Mr. Trefalden smiled in his pleasantest manner.

"I do think," said he, "that you are the most foolish fellow in the world. If I don't make haste to tie your money up, you will ruin yourself, rich as you are!"

"But what's the use of being rich if I may

not enjoy my wealth in my own way?" laughed Saxon, delighted to have carried his point.

"Your way is a very irrational way," replied the lawyer, taking a slip of paper from his desk and writing upon it in a clear engrossing hand; "almost as irrational as that of the poor sailors who make sandwiches of their bank notes and bread-and-butter. But I suppose I must forgive you for this once; and, after all, the loss of fifty-nine thousand is better than the loss of a quarter of a million. There, put that in your purse, and see that your devoted friend signs it on the blank line at the bottom."

"What is it?"

"A promissory note for the money. He will perhaps offer you an ordinary receipt on the part of the firm; but this, if signed in the name of the firm, will answer the purpose much better. What—going already?"

Saxon explained that Greatorex wanted the cash before one o'clock.

"You have removed the 'stop' from Drummond's, I suppose?"

"Not yet. I will call there as I go home."

"And Mr. Greatorex has given you back your first cheque?"

"I don't know. I think we left it on the breakfast-table."

Mr. Trefalden bit his lip.

"Upon my soul, Saxon," he said, "you deserve to be fleeced by every sharper who can get his hand within reach of a feather of you! Go home and find that cheque before you dream of removing your injunction; and if you can't find it, give them a note of the number and amount, in case of its being presented for payment."

Saxon laughed, and promised obedience; but declared there was no danger.

"And you will still keep your promise of signing away no more money without consulting me?"

"Implicitly."

"Then good-bye till Thursday."

Saxon sprang down the stairs whistling a shrill Swiss air, and was gone in a moment; and Mr. Trefalden's face, as he listened, grew dark, and hard, and cold, as if it were changing into granite.

"Fool!" he muttered, fiercely. "As eager to

ruin himself as are others to ruin him ! I should
be mad to hold back now. I have waited, and
watched, and let him go his own way long
enough; but my turn has come at last, and I
mean to seize it."

"If you please, sir," said Mr. Keckwitch,
putting his head suddenly in at the door, "Mr.
Behrens called about ten minutes ago, and said
he'd come again at two."

"Very well," replied the lawyer, wearily.
"Bring me Mr. Behrens' deed-box."

And then he sat for a long time with the box
unopened before him, and his head resting on his
hands.

CHAPTER XXIII.

THE HOLE IN WILLIAM TREFALDEN'S ARMOUR.

THE man who has a purpose to achieve, or a secret to hide, should never make an enemy. It is his obvious policy to shun that disaster as sedulously as an expectant bridegroom shuns the conscription, a débutante the small-pox, or a railway director the possible horrors of an excursion train. But the wisest cannot always be wise; and the wariest are apt now and then to omit some little precaution whereby the dread catastrophe against which they have so long been building up their defences, might have been averted after all. Thetis, when she dipped Achilles in the seven-fold river, forgot the heel by which she held him, and left it vulnerable for the fatal arrow. Imperial Cæsar put aside for future reading the paper that would have saved him from assassination. Henri Quatre—he of the valiant heart, to whom nothing seemed impossible—neglected alike his own presentiments, and the prayers of those who loved him, when he went forth to his doom in the Rue de la Ferronière. These things are common. We read of them in the records of almost every famous crime, or sudden catastrophe. The "complete steel" has some weak point of junction which the foeman's blade finds out. The conspirator drops a paper, and the plot which was to subvert a dynasty recoils on the heads of the plotters. The cleverest alibi breaks down in some minute particular which no one had the wit to foresee. A little more prudence was alone needed to ensure quite opposite results—a little better closing of the rivets of the gorget, or the seams of the pocket, or the incidents of the story; but the precaution that would have made all safe, was precisely that precaution which happened to be neglected.

William Trefalden had both a purpose to achieve, and a secret to hide, and he was not insensible to the inconveniences that might arise from the ill-will of his fellow-men; but he had made two enemies, and those two enemies were the two greatest errors of his life. He had never attempted to be what is called "a popular man." He had none of that apparent frankness and buoyancy of manner necessary to the part; but he especially desired to be well spoken of. He *was* well spoken of, and had acquired that sort of reputation which is, above all others, the most valuable to a professional man—a reputation for sagacity, and prosperity; and prosperity, be it remembered, is the seal of merit. But, having achieved so much, and being on the high road to certain other achievements, the nature of which was as yet known only to himself, he ought to have abstained at any cost from awaking the enmity of two such men as Abel Keckwitch and Laurence Greatorex. It would have been better for him if he had denied himself the satisfaction of punishing his head clerk that memorable evening in March, and been content only to dodge him in the shade of the doorway. It would have been better if, knowing himself to be the destined Jason, he had even suffered Laurence Greatorex to carry off that noble slice from the Golden

Fleece, which was represented by Saxon's first cheque. But he had followed neither of these prudent courses. He despised the clerk, he was irritated against the banker, and he never even asked himself how they were disposed towards him in return. They both hated him; but had he known this, it is probable that he would have been equally indifferent to the fact. Not to know it— not even to have given it a thought, one way or the other—was a great oversight; and that oversight was the one hole in William Trefalden's armour.

Mr. Abel Keckwitch was a very respectable man. He lodged in the house of a gaunt widow who lived in a small back street at Pentonville; and his windows commanded a thriving churchyard. He paid his rent with scrupulous regularity; he went to church every Sunday morning; he took in the Weekly Observer; he kept a cat; and he played the violoncello. He had done all these things for the last thirty years, and he did them advisedly; for Mr. Keckwitch was of a methodical temperament, and loved to carry on the unprofessional half of his existence in a groove of

the strictest routine. Having started in life with
the determination of being eminently respectable,
he had modelled himself after his own matter-of-
fact ideal, and cut his tastes according to his
judgment. His cat and his violoncello were cases
in point. He would have preferred a dog; but
he made choice of the cat, because puss looked
more domestic, and reflected the quiet habits of
her master. In like manner, Mr. Keckwitch entertained a secret leaning towards the concertina;
but he yielded this point in favour of the superior
respectability of the violoncello. And it cannot
be denied that Mr. Keckwitch was right. A
more respectable possession than a violoncello for
a single man, can hardly be conceived. It is the
very antithesis to all that is light and frivolous.
It leads to no conviviality. It neither inclines
its owner to quadrille parties, like the cornet-à-
pistons, nor to cold gin-and-water, like the flute;
and it lends itself to amateur psalmody after a
manner unequalled in dreariness by any other
instrument. It was Mr. Keckwitch's custom to
practise for an hour every evening after tea; and
in the summer he did it with the windows open,

which afflicted the neighbourhood with an universal melancholy. At these times his landlady would shed tears for her departed husband, and declare that "it was beautiful, and she felt all the better for it;" and the photographer next door, who was a low-spirited young man, and read Byron, would shut himself up in his dark room, and indulge in thoughts of suicide.

Such was the placid and irreproachable tenor of Mr. Abel Keckwitch's home life. It suited his temperament, and it gratified his ambition. He knew that he inspired the lodging-house bosom with confidence, and the parochial authorities with esteem. The pew-opener curtsied to him, and the churchwardens nodded to him affably in the street. In short, Pentonville regarded him as a thoroughly respectable man.

Scarcely less methodical was the other—the professional—half of this respectable man's career. He was punctuality itself, and hung his hat up in William Trefalden's office every morning at nine with as much exactitude as the clock announced the hour. At one, he repaired to an eating-house in High Holborn, where he had dined at the same cost, and from the same dishes, for the last two-and-twenty years. Don Quixote's diet before he took to knight-errantry was not more monotonous; but instead of the "pigeon extra-ordinary on Sundays," Mr. Keckwitch dined on that day at his landlady's table, and stipulated for pudding. At two, he resumed his seat at the office desk; and, when there was no particular pressure of work, went home to his cat and his violoncello at half-past six. At certain seasons, however, Mr. Keckwitch and his fellow-clerks were almost habitually detained for an hour or an hour and a half over-time, and thereby grew the richer; for William Trefalden was a pro-sperous man, and paid his labourers fairly.

So sober, so steady, so plodding was the head clerk's daily round of occupation. He fattened upon it, and grew asthmatic as the years went by. No one would have dreamed, to look into his dull eyes and stolid face, that he could be other than the veriest machine that ever drove a quill; but he was nothing of the kind. He was an invaluable clerk; and William Trefalden knew his worth precisely. His head was as clear

as his voice was husky; his memory was pro-
digious; and for all merely technical purposes
he was as good a lawyer as Trefalden himself.
He entertained certain views, however, with
regard to his own field of action, which by no
means accorded with those of his employer. He
liked to know everything; and he conceived that
it was his right, as Mr. Trefalden's head clerk,
to establish a general supervision of the whole
of that gentleman's professional and private
affairs. He also deemed it to be in some sort
his duty to find out that which was withheld from
him, and regarded every reservation as a personal affront. That Mr. Trefalden should keep
certain papers for his own reading; should
answer certain letters with his own hand; and
should sometimes remain in his private room for
long hours after he and the others were dismissed, preparing unknown documents, and even
holding conferences with strangers upon subjects that never filtered through to the outer
office, were offences which it was not in Mr.
Keckwitch's nature to forgive. Nor were these
all the wrongs of which he had to complain. It

was William Trefalden's pleasure to keep his
private life and his private affairs strictly to himself. No man knew whether he was married or
single. No man knew how or where he lived.
His practice was large and increasing, and the
proceeds thereof were highly lucrative. Mr.
Keckwitch had calculated them many a time, and
could give a shrewd guess at the amount of his
master's annual income. But what did he do
with this money? How did he invest it? Did
he invest it at all? Was it lent out at usurious
interest, in quarters not to be named indiscreetly?
Or launched in speculations that would not bear
the light of day? Or gambled away at the tables
of some secret hell, in the purlieus of the Hay-
market or Leicester Square? Or was the lawyer
a mere vulgar miser, after all, hoarding his good
gold in the cracks and crevices of some ruinous
old house, the address of which he guarded as
jealously as if it were the key to his wealth?

Here was the mystery of mysteries; here was
the ark of William Trefalden's secret; here was
the one thing which Abel Keckwitch's whole soul
was bent on discovering.

Possessed by that innate curiosity which acted as the leaven to his phlegmatic temperament, the head clerk had for years pondered over this mystery; lain in wait for it; scented round it from all sides; and, in a certain dogged way, resented it. But since that evening of the second of March, he had fixed upon it with a vindictive tenacity as deadly as the coil of the boa. He saw, or believed he saw, in this thing a weapon wherewith to chastise the man who had dared to find him out, and call him spy; and upon this one object he concentrated the whole force of his sluggish but powerful will. For Abel Keckwitch was a hater after Byron's own heart, and loved to nurse his wrath, and brood upon it, and keep it warm. He never passed that doorway in Chancery Lane without rehearsing the whole scene in his mind. He remembered every insulting word that William Trefalden had hurled at him in those three or four moments. He still felt the iron blow—the breathless shock—the burning sense of rage and humiliation; and these things rankled day by day in the respectable bosom of Abel Keckwitch, and were each day farther and farther from being forgiven and forgotten.

The secret, however, remained as dark as ever. He had fancied once or twice of late that he was on the verge of some discovery ; but he had each time found himself misled by his suspicions, and as far off as ever from the goal.

Hope deferred and wrath long cherished began at length to tell upon Mr. Keckwitch's health and spirits. He became morose and abstracted. He gave up practising the violoncello. He lost his appetite for the diurnal meats of High Holborn, and his relish for the leaders that he was wont to devour with his cheese. And he forgot to take notice of his cat. His landlady and his fellow-clerks saw and marvelled at the change, and the soul of the one-eyed waiter who received Mr. Keckwitch's daily obolus, was perplexed within him ; but none dared to question him. They observed him from afar off, as the Greeks looked upon Achilles sitting sullenly beside his ships, and canvassed his mood " with bated breath and whispering humbleness."

This went on for weeks ; and then, all at once,

the tide turned, and Mr. Keckwitch became himself again. An idea had occurred to him—a
bright idea, by the light of which he distinctly
saw the path to success opening out before him.
He only wondered that he had not thought of it
sooner.

CHAPTER XXIV.

SAXON TREFALDEN was in buoyant spirits that afternoon as he wandered to and fro among the intricate platforms of the Waterloo-Bridge station, and watched the coming and going of the trains. He had plenty of time; for he was a very inexperienced traveller, and, in his anxiety to be punctual, had come half an hour too soon. But his mind was full of pleasant thoughts, and he enjoyed the life and bustle of the place with as much zest as if the whole scene were a comedy played for his amusement.

He was very happy. He thought, as he went strolling up and down, that he had scarcely ever felt so happy in his life.

In the first place, he had that day received a letter from Pastor Martin—a long, loving, pious

letter, filled with sweet home news, and benevolent projects about good things to be done in
the valley of Domleschg. The remittance which
he had dispatched the very day after he drew
his first cheque had been distributed among the
poor of the neighbouring parishes: the organ
that he had sent out a fortnight since had
arrived, and the workmen were busy with it
daily: the farm buildings at Rotzberg were being
repaired, and the three meadows down by the
river-side, that had been so long for sale, were
now bought in Saxon's name, and added to the
little demesne. The pigeons, too, had a new
pigeon-house; and the spotted cow had calved;
and the thrushes that built last year in the great
laurel down at the end of the garden, had again
made their nest in the branches of the same tree.
These were trifles; but to Saxon, who loved his
far-away home, his native valley, and all the
surroundings of his boyhood with the passionate
enthusiasm of a mountaineer, they were trifles
infinitely precious and delightful. And besides
all this, the letter ended with a tender blessing
that had rested upon his heart ever since he read

it, and seemed to hallow all the sunshine of the
April day.

Then, in the second place, he had that morning enjoyed the supreme luxury of doing good.
William Trefalden had, it is true, affirmed that
the hours of Greatorex and Greatorex were
numbered, and that Saxon's fifty-nine thousands
could only interpose a brief delay between the
bankers and their ruin; but Laurence Greatorex,
with the crisp bank-notes in his hand, had assured him that this sum, by renewing their credit
and tiding them over the present emergency,
was certain salvation to the firm. Taking it on
the whole, this matter of the cheque had been
sufficiently disagreeable. It had · shown the
banker's disposition from an unfavourable point
of view, and to withdraw from even a part of
his rash promise had been a source of humiliation to Saxon. Perhaps, too, the young man
could not help liking his friend somewhat less
than before; and this is at all times a painful
feeling. Himself one of nature's own gentlemen, he shrank instinctively from all that was
coarse and mercenary; and he could not shut his

eyes to the fact that Greatorex had shown himself
to be both. However, it had ended pleasantly.
Saxon had saved his friend, and the banker had
not only overwhelmed him with professions of
gratitude, but given him a proper acknowledg-
ment for the money, so that William Trefalden's
promissory note (which Saxon knew he should
never have produced, though he had lost every
penny by the omission) was happily not needed
after all.

And in the third place, he was going into the
country for a week or ten days. That was the
last and best of all! After five weeks of feverish
London life—five long, dazzling, breathless, wonderful weeks—he felt his heart leap at the
thought of the free, fresh air, and open sky. He
longed to be up and out again at grey dawn,
scenting the morning air. He longed to feel
the turf under his feet. Above all, he longed
to practise the art of horsemanship in some
more favourable locality than the yard of the
riding-school, or the crowded manège of Rotten
Row. To this end, he had a couple of thorough-
breds and a groom with him, and had just seen

the animals safely disposed of in a horse-box,
ready to join the train as soon as it was backed
into the station.

So Saxon was in great spirits, and went round
and about, looking at the book-stalls and the
hurrying passengers, and thinking what a charming thing it was to have youth, riches, friends,
and all the world of books and art before one!
There were, in truth, a great many half-formed
projects floating about his brain just now—vague
pictures of a yachting tour in the Mediterranean;
visions of Rome, and Naples, and the isles of
Greece; glimpses of the Nile, and the Pyramids,
and even of the white domes of Jerusalem. For
some of these schemes Lord Castletowers was
answerable; but, let the foreground be what it
might, the familiar snow peaks of the Rhætian
Alps closed in the distance of every wondrous
landscape that Saxon's vivid imagination bodied
forth. He had no thought of wandering into
Italy without first re-visiting the valley of
Domleschg; and still less did he ever dream of
making his permanent home away from that still,
primitive, untrodden place. But he had projects

about that also, and meant some day to build
a beautiful commodious château (not so large,
but much more beautiful than the Count
Planta's), and to rebuild the church, and throw
a new bridge over the Rhine, and erect model
cottages, and make every one happy around
him.

"Well, what is it?" said an authoritative voice.
"Anything the matter?"

Saxon was looking at the red-and-gold backs
of a long row of Traveller's Guides on a book-
stand close by, and the voice broke in abruptly
on the pleasant reverie which their titles had
suggested. He turned, and saw a lady, a railway
guard, and a burly-looking official with a pen
behind his ear, standing at the door of an empty
second-class carriage of the up-train which had
discharged its freight of passengers three or four
minutes ago.

The guard touched his cap.

"Lady's lost her ticket, sir," he replied, with a
knowing twinkle of the eye.

"I know I had it when the train stopped at
Weybridge," said the lady. "I took it out from

my purse, because I thought the guard was going
to ask to see it."

Her voice trembled a little as she said this,
stooping forward into the carriage all the while,
in search of the missing ticket.

The burly official drew his hand across his
mouth, and coughed doubtfully.

"Where did you take it from, miss?" he
asked.

"From Sedgebrook station."

The name came familiarly to Saxon's ear, for
it happened that Sedgebrook was precisely the
point to which Lord Castletowers had directed
him to take his own ticket.

"Humph!   Well, Salter, I suppose you've
searched the carriage thoroughly?"

"Quite thoroughly, sir," replied the guard.

The official went through the form of peering
into it himself, and said :—

"Then, miss, I'm afraid there's no help for it."

"Shall I have to pay the fare a second time?"
asked the lady, nervously.

"You'll have to pay it from Exeter—the point
where the train started from."

"From Exeter? But I only came from Sedgebrook!"

"Can't help that, miss. Those are our regulations. Any passenger, unable to produce his ticket on alighting, must pay his full fare from the point of departure. This train comes from Exeter, and from Exeter you must pay. There hangs our table of by-laws. You can see it for yourself."

Her face was turned towards Saxon now, as she stood by the carriage door looking from the one man to the other. It was a very young face, quite childlike in its appealing timidity, and as pale as a lily.

"Thank you," she said, hurriedly, "I don't want to see it. I am quite satisfied with what you say. How much will it be?"

"One pound five."

The pale face became scarlet, and the childlike eyes filled with sudden tears.

"Oh, dear!" she said, tremulously, "what shall I do? I have not nearly so much money as that!"

Saxon had seen that she was poorly dressed,

and he knew, as well as if he had looked into it, that her slender purse could ill spare even the paltry three shillings and sixpence from Sedgebrook to London. His hand had been in his waistcoat pocket half-a-dozen times already, and was only withdrawn empty because he felt that it would be a simple impertinence to interpose. But now he could bear it no longer.

"May I be permitted, madam," he said, bowing to the young girl as profoundly as if she were a princess of the blood royal, "to arrange this matter for you?"

And he slipped her fare into the hand of the guard.

The blush deepened painfully upon her cheek.

"I—I thank you, sir," she faltered. "I thank you very much. Will you be good enough to give me your card, that I may know where to send the money?"

Saxon felt in his pockets, looked in his purse, and found that he had not the vestige of a card about him. At this moment a bell rang on the opposite platform, and a porter whom he had entrusted with his railway rug and the task

of securing him a seat, came running breathlessly up.

"Train's just a going, sir," said he. "You've
not a minute to lose."

So Saxon bowed again, stammered something
about being "very sorry," and vanished from the
scene.

Just as he had taken his seat, however, and
the train had begun to move, the guard appeared
at the window, tossed in a card, said something
which was lost in the shrill shriek of the driver's
whistle, and dropped out of sight.

Saxon picked up the card, which was rather
small for a lady's use, and read :—

Miss Rivière,

Photographic Colourist,

6, *Brudenell Terrace, Camberwell.*

"Poor little thing!" he said to himself, with a
pitying smile, "does she suppose that I will send
to her for the trumpery money!"

And then he was about to throw it out of the

window ; but checked himself, looked at it again, and put it in his waistcoat pocket instead.

"She was very pretty," thought he ; "and her voice was very sweet.   How glad I am that I had no card about me !"

END OF VOL. I.

BRADBURY, EVANS, AND CO., PRINTERS, WHITEFRIARS.

UNIVERSITY OF ILLINOIS-URBANA

3 0112 045828420

www.ingramcontent.com/pod-product-compliance
Lightning Source LLC
Chambersburg PA
CBHW031339070726
47496CB00017B/1301